S0-EGE-602

JANE —

FOR MY FAVORITE
SO WOMAN !

ALOHA

5-25-23

ANNOTATED NOTES IN TIME

EARTHS

AN
INVISIBLE
PRESENCE

JON W. SHAW

FIRST PHASE

Reader reviews: Tom Brockley

Annotated Notes in Time, EARTHS – book 1
Has it all, adventure, history, geography, comedy, science, love and suspense. Just when his young travelers get accustomed to leaping centuries of time, their quest transports the seekers to a more incredible universe.

Frank Rose

5.0 out of 5 stars <u>A heartwarming story combining family values, magic, time travel, and much more! Go for it!</u>

EARTHS

Copyright © 2018 by Jon W. Shaw
This is a work of fiction. All that is contained within is possible and probable. The writings are a product of the authors thought as a possibility of past and future events. Any resemblances to events or locales are intended- passed, living or future.
Indie published by   Jon W. Shaw

ISBN: 9798569724710

Cover design: Olivia, Lizzy & Katy Shaw

First Edition October 2018
Second Edition October 2019
Third Edition October 2019
Fourth Edition October 2020

If you would like to bother the author:
nextaddress100@gmail.com
Please do.

EARTHS

Copyright © 2018 by Jon W. Shaw
All rights reserved.
No part of this book may be reproduced in any form or by any electronic or mechanical means, including information storage and retrieval systems, without written permission from the author, except for the use of brief quotations in a book review.

Olivia, Elizabeth, Katy

My Three Impossible Girls

My Friends,
who have
exceeded every
definition of the word.

FOREWORD

I am fully aware of the constant testing timeline at CERN.
I needed to create a structured time of 'phasing' for the framing of
different parts of each book.

All these elements are mathematically possible, I merely
added a fun human side.

This interest in other
worlds was ignited by my uncle Don Shaw who
worked for Howard Hughes.
His stories always had me riveted!
J W S

Schrodinger Expression:
This is what one of his theory looks like on paper

$$i\hbar\frac{\partial}{\partial t}\Psi(\mathbf{r},t) = \left[\frac{-\hbar^2}{2\mu}\nabla^2 + V(\mathbf{r},t)\right]\Psi(\mathbf{r},t)$$

Google Scholar

Defiantly not most folks fun side, somewhere there's a cat
that we can't decide if it's alive or …

Other stories by, **Jon W. Shaw:**

<u>Annotated Notes in Time</u>

Book 1. <u>EARTHS-</u>

Invisible Presence

Book 2. <u>LINGERING EARTHS-</u>

Book 3. <u>ENDURING EARTHS-</u>

A Propitious Presence

STEMMING TROUBLE #1

Science Adventure

<u>In A Blue Moon</u> #1

Science Adventure

Due 2021:

Artificial Horizon #2

<u>After a Blue moon #2</u>

<u>Willing Players</u>

(English-Gaelic)

~ Dr. Johnstone - Head of Physics division

~ Dr. Rym Sachs - Father of Tayas

~ Dr. Qwe Rtyuiop-Husband of Tayas (es) father of
the Three

~ Dr. Tayas Sachs - Rtyuiop - Mother of
Tamra, Carisa, and Lyka

~ Tamra - Tamra Sachs

~ Lyka - Coltach Sachs

~ Carisa - Uisge Sachs

— Merlin - Ambrosius

~ Nyneve - Lady of the Lake

~ Emily - from T-3

~ Lisa - from T-3

~ Paul - Clairvoyant on T-3

~ Ozbetin (Oz) — lab tech - Tamra's b-friend

~ Athena - Sister of Ozbetin

~ Artemis (Art) — Boyfriend, of Athena

~ Jim ~ Boyfriend of Carisa

~ Rex ~ Boyfriend of Lyka

~ Samantha (Sam) — family friend of Athena

~ Dr. Mera - gifted traveler — a friend of Rym

Willing Players

- **Alda** - friend of Merlin's, Sterling Castle kitchen worker
- **Rune** - husband of Alda - kick but guy
    - **Max** - Mercenary, sailor
    - **Anthony** - Time hitchhiker, General for Fidalac
    - **Fidalac** - wants to be Emperor of many worlds

Continuums of EARTHS

(Only the ones visited by the three sisters)

L - 1 The earth here and now

L - 2. The time of Merlyn on a different earth

L - 3 The future of this earth

L - 4 The future time on an Emily earth

L - 5 The time on a different Water earth

L - 6 Water earth x Û….

Contents

Prologue

"Having a known as a fact, water to fish, oxygen to humans.
Frequencies are portals to
subtly different universes."

-Dr. Johnstone-

Tamra was asking for help. Two of her close friends had come over to see if they could shed any light on her latest wonders. Dinner was an easy lure for the evening, Tayas always felt at home here in her friends eclectic Geneva apartment. Her other guest Dr. Rym, was out on the deck, enjoying a lazy warm summer evening attending the Bar-B-Q.

Tayas, was reflexively reaching for a salsa dip with her chips by a game the two girls were concentrating on... well in all truth, one was.

She was really giving it a lot of thought, but it was the pleasant BBQ aromas drifting in through the french doors that were winning over her concentration.

This chess game was kinda hard to play due to the added third dimension. The sideways effect on the player is to not be overly chatty.

Almost contentedly waiting for her turn, Tamra was idly cataloging her surroundings and had to outwardly admit....

"Ya think I should do some work on this apartment? Can't expect to get a guy ta feel comfortable around here with all my girly stuff."

Turning back to Tayas for an opinion on what she thought about the whole idea, she was awarded a half response,

"Hmm…well…sure…ok…."

Visibly frustrated, softly cuffing her game opponent,

"Hay u' punk! I have guy problems we need to talk about, forget the game…"

Tayas then decided to socially revive herself , with a natural smile a dentist would be envious of,

"Ok, I think so…"

Tamra quizzically asking, "You think what?"

Tayas standing up, pointing and directing,

"You should repaint and change out some of this furniture; I'll take the bookcase it's too old and dated for a single girl…."

Tamra roiling her eyes, flopping back on the couch,

"I didn't say anything about painting, but I guess mauve everywhere is a bit much.

The airplane noise here is enough to make me search out a new place anyway, what do you think about a move?"

Tayas was starting to answer when Dr. Rym, stepped in from outside,

"Tri-tip is ready… your turn to set the table…"

The house phone started ringing, Tamra hopped up absently saying,

"All right, ll'me get the phone first…(she still actually had a land line!)

"Hello? … That's really weird; It's for you Dr. Rym… it sounds like a recording?"

Taking the phone, almost instantly his face registered trepidation-"

"Yes…Elderberry…" Listening very intently for only a few moments, then quickly ending the call,

"Ladies, I must be going, Dr. Johnstone might have just vanished from the face of this earth!"

Chapter One

"Wonder what all that stuff was about…Elderberry?"

Tayas "It's an activation phrase, we use em there in the lab. It brings up a prerecorded statement."

Dr. Rym's hasty exit had both girls thinking, but it was their original conversation that brought Tayas back to the moment, her hand halfway to the salsa again, thoughtfully pausing,

"You don't even have a boyfriend; maybe you should work on that one-first."

Tamra was about to launch into a rebuttal, but it was the phone ringing again, hoping up with a sly smile at Tayas,

"I'll bet that's a man now…"

With a quick steep to the kitchen and answering with a very friendly voice,

"Good evening…"

"Hi, could I speak with Tamra, this is Ozbetin."

With a fast smile, "That's me!"

Unexpectedly, she now was delighted on two fronts:

One; she now could tell Tayas, I told you so.

Two; she was holding herself back a little, didn't want him to think that she was thrilled. (Sometimes attractive girls have a difficult time getting intelligent young men to call) With small pleasantries aside, his true intention was to ask if she would accompany him to an office festivity of some importance. Tamra very coolly accepted and was off the phone and in Taya's face,

"That's the one I was going to tell you about, Ha!"

Tayas, with a smile was inwardly very happy for her. They'd been good friends since early adulthood and shared a lot in the past. They had met while attending College and Graduate schools together. She came to ETH Zurich University from a very nice family that had adopted her at three years of age, with a considerable amount of political presence in Barcelona.

After a little chat, it was the phone again, Tamra jumped up, thinking Ozbetin wanted to add an idea from the last conversation. So, she answered the phone with a small sexy soft tone,

"Halloo…"

"Yes, Tamra? Dr. Rym here,"
A little embarrassed….changing up tones,

"Yes, ah…. Hi Dr. Rym, what's-u up to?"

"Everything is fine here, and I will fill you both in back at your place. I was wondering if I could bring someone else along?"

Tamra instantly knew who it was, "Sure, is he tall, dark, handsome and single?"

Rym "He's all those things except single."

"Ok, if you must, we'll see you when we see you."

Dr. Rym & Dr. Qwe arriving at Tamra's building, stepping out of the tube, headed for the elevator. Knocking on apt. I-5. Qwe, headed straight for his wife, hugging her a little too much, in a squeaky voice,

"Woo-hang on! We just saw each other this morning. I love you too!"
He still was emotionally charged from the event earlier.

"No, you hang on, (kiss) I really don't know how to begin, your dad can help me out I hope."

Rym "Yes, and for your information dear daughter, I know you will ask… he is just fine."

Wondering, with half confused smiles from the two girls,

Rym "Lets pick-up with dinner where we left off shall we?"

Tamra, a bit precocious, never letting too much bother her, lightheartedly standing with arms crossed and tapping her toe,

"Can someone fill us in, and by the way, I need hugs from the men present if they want anything on their plate…"

The man folk, of course, we're happy to oblige, and dinner was on-again.

Tayas naturality had a number of questions, Rym looked at Qwe with a knowing smile.

"Ok husband of mine, tell me what this is all about hum…?"

"You won't believe what just happened, I hardly believe it or how to explain it…. I was static, like on tv a little while ago. You'll have to ask your father for any suitable solid answer. "

Rym had other things in mind, but he started to explain,

"Yes, this is extremely sensitive, and I know Qwe, Tayas, and our hostess won't take this to anyone else. We all work at the same location, and we know many amazing, sometimes hard to except, wonders are born across the street at the Hadron Collider.

This unanticipated occurrence is a phenomenon, something that is very new to Dr. Johnstone and myself, so that's all I'll say for the moment. What I will say now is, I would like to finish what is in front of me before it goes artic for the second time tonight!"

Tamra briefly clapping her hands together with a relived expression,

"Wow you guys! … That was so close! No offense Dr.'s, I was starting to think the evening talk was going to descend into all things scientific…let's put a lid on all that crap!
I had a reason I invited Tayas over and I need her ideas, I am trying to get a new guy."

Small laughs,

Tamra "I can tell Tayas is ready to explode with questions. In no way can you start with anything to do with science… well, maybe there is some guy science you can help with, ok… hum?"

Chapter Two

Dr. Rym hurriedly slid his overcoat on, standing in front of the closet door mirror looking at his reflection a bit puzzled. Trying to reconstruct possible options. Accepting the fact that he and his colleague had stumbled onto something that might make any 'Time travel' possibility come true. Dr. J & Dr. Rym's work had branched off and led them down a very unexpected alley of Theoretical Physics.

Heading for the door with a quick step past his daughter and friend,

"My apologies ladies, something is very wrong at the laboratory!"

The two girls looked a little concerned, and they started to ask,

Rym "I'll call when I get there."

Waiting impatiently for the elevator, stepping out quickly to the next transport across the lobby. Reaching for the tube panel directory, pressing the "CERN lab complex."

An extremely futuristic six place tube transport car was waiting, stepping in a clear shield slid into place, and he was on his way. He knew it would take only three minutes to arrive.

Bearing in mind what he & Dr. Johnstone had previously experienced, a number of different variables presented themselves.

Arriving at the CERN tube platform, hastily stepping out of the tube, down the hall and into his laboratory.

He was met with a welcome sight, Dr. Johnstone and Dr. Qwe were comfortably sitting, reviewing what had just happened.

He was deeply relieved, although still feeling very concerned and very uncertain.

Dr. Johnstone was considerably excited.

"Dr. it was a quasi-start that I don't understand yet, I'm thinking on that. I placed the crystal in the test rack only to demonstrate for Dr. Qwe, as I was explaining our theory to him, we started to phase!"

Rym "You two go on ahead, I'm going to check on some of our recording stations."

All this was very novel for both men, and both men were determined to fathom what other random possibly could have happened. Rym started a wide-ranging review of all the data and equipment that were available to their unexpected avenue of research.

Dr. J with Dr. Qwe,

"I know you have been introduced to the 'parallel earth theories.' Also, the different timelines that may be associated with them in regard to the theoretical postulates that have been proven in most instances."

Qwe "Yes, it's still of great interest to me and a lot of other possibilities years ago at M. I. T. and still…."

Rym from across the busy lab interrupted abruptly,

"Dr. J maybe we should let him decide…"

Rym stepped over and Dr. J turned to confer in quiet,

"This is evidently not as uncommon as we have deliberated in the past. I think we should proceed slowly, but I also think we need to introduce someone else."

Dr. J "I agree with you Dr. it would be wise to let another party know the whole picture, we might be taken again, and none would know!"

Rym turning to include the third Dr. in their group,

"Qwe, first of all we would hope, if in fact you would be open to an idea that we can now personally verify, that would take all the things you learned in Theory, straight into reality."

Qwe "That's the reason of why I'm here. So many things change so fast, I'd like to be part of whatever you have been looking at."

Dr. J and Rym were satisfied.

"Let's sit an talk, we've done more than just look. The two of us have in fact found that we can travel to other worlds, and in all truth, different times in history!

One aspect of quantum mechanics is that certain observations cannot be predicted absolutely. When Max Planck won the Nobel prize way back in 1918, he introduced a new range of possible observations, each with a wildly different sub-sets and probabilities.

According to the M W I (many-worlds interpretation) each of these possible observations corresponds to a different mathematical universe. Suppose a six-sided die is thrown and that the result of the throw corresponds to a quantum mechanics observable. All six possible ways the die can fall correspond to six different universes. Tegmark…"

Qwe interjected "He was one of my professors at MIT, enjoyed it."

Dr. J carried straight on,

"Oh, well good…. Argues that a level three multiverses does not contain any more possibilities in the Hubble volume than a level one or the level two multiverse.

In effect, all the different earths created by 'splits' or 'bubbles' in a level three multiverse with the same physical constants can be found in some Hubble volumes in a level one multiverse.

Tegmark writes that,

"The only difference between level one and level three, that is where your doppelgängers* reside. In level one they live elsewhere in good old three-dimensional space. In level three they live on another quantum branch in infinite-dimensional Hilbert Space**"

**[Hilbert space generalizes the notion of Euclidean space. It extends the methods of vector algebra and calculus from the two-dimensional Euclidean plane and three-dimensional space to spaces with any finite or infinite number of dimensions.]

"These are things you know. Please understand, Rym & I have in our position a most unique historical treasure. I'll add unworldly, only for the fact we are not sure which world it was issued from."

Qwe was almost bursting,

"How… what….are you suggesting I can pick a world and go?"

Rym & Dr. J lightly laughed

Dr. J "No is the simple answer. Yes, is the complicated one."

Qwe was silently attuning his next question,

Dr. J "We know what you feel right now, but let's stay on track to investigate our sources.

First; We have a 'crystal,'

Second; We now know when and where it was found,

Third; The area and time has been historically associated with magic."

Qwe "Magic! Like ferry dust, spells, turning your enemies into frogs, that sort of thing?"

Rym smiling broadly

"If you recall, that was where the doppelgängers fit in. Any conceivable parallel universe at level four subsumes all other ensembles, of course in level five there some mild disagreements. Remember, and we think this is a key factor. "Entanglement" you remember Professor Boles spinning coins, and Einstein's "spooky theories at a distance?*""

Qwe "Yes, spin two like coins, and even at any distance they will land with their opposite faces showing up."

Rym "We think that this crystal has a home, and it wants to balance itself. But I'm splintering off from what I intended to tell you. A chance occurrence that Dr. J & I have had is going to explain a lot, so let's not explore more theory now at this point."

Qwe yielded, "Ok, al-right let's start at the top, -wait a second I was a blur, like static on tv! Just a few minutes ago!"

Rym "Yes, but now you feel as if it never happened, yes?"

Dr. J couldn't wait,

"History first! our crystal was found near a small village, 'Alva' about 30 km northwest of Sterling, Scotland"

Qwe "That's odd, I was unaware of that type of geological occurrence in the UK of that nature."

"Not so, young man, how is your English folk lore? Let me just touch on one such event. King Arthur, Lancelot, Merlin.

I am sure, names you are familiar with from 'Camelot's' enduring lore. King Arthur's lead councilor and magi, 'Merlyn' took up residence in some such of a 'crystal cave.'

His personal history is of course somewhat ambiguous to say the least, but we are in an earlier line of thought, let's work through the original first.

Dr. Qwe was attentively listening,

"The engine behind this mystery we have stumbled on, is exclusively involved with our association inside the small loop with the Hadron Collider. Our offices being located inside the SPS, ATLAS small satellite ring, then of course the 27km LHC around all of that.

Tesla found that some forms of energy is in an ambient state, in a bubble so to speak. He was able to move energy without any physical means, no wires, we think that is what is happening here.

When they are reaching for the incident that requires larger amounts of energy in the quest to reproduce Black Holes or smash led protons together. High draw events close to that index is the key, it's all in that energy that is amassed in one quantum place."

Rym noticing Qwe,

"Qwe, you do feel all right?"

"Now it kinda feels like I have been left in the M. R. I. machine way to long"

"Hum, good way to put it, we will follow this discussion a little farther on at Tamra's. Let's head over that way now, I know she and especially Tayas will have questions abounding!"

***Hosting events that Einstein termed as "spooky" Difficult even for him to except, as well as an 'Expanding universe.'

Chapter Three

Qwe found himself at his office door quite early the next morning. His night was one that most all of us humans would disagree with, filled with anxious thoughts of things unknown, over and over. On his arrival, finding Dr. J still transcribing all data that was available, appraising Qwe,

Dr. J, "Have you any side effects?"
"None but the lack of sleep!"

"Well, yes, yes to be expected, I would request all questions to be held until Dr. Rym arrives…"
Qwe was not to be overly anxious for long,

"Bonjour fella't directors."

(For the reader; English and French are the two languages spoken at CERN.)

Rym noted Qwe looking ruffled as he sat alone with so many questions and nobody around to answer. Clapping his hands together in the cool morning office air, smiling,

"Well, let's step into it shall we Dr. J?"
Gathering in the conferencing annex, Dr. J assuming the lead,

"In addressing all of the newly acquired available data, I have found the anomaly which has preceded Rym & myself in antecedent transverses. In all, two times…."

"Wait…Wait for just one-second…"
All of a sudden, Qwe didn't feel alone anymore.

"The two of you have experienced what I was feeling yesterday?"

Rym "Yes, but in the full meaning of the word, consuming!"

He continued on,

"We have twice landed in another Time. Both are in the slightly distant past of this earth, or quite possibly a different earth entirely. In the primary event we were only present for two hours thankfully, we had no way to start a fire or any food. On the second phasing, we were a little more prepared and we were out for five of our 24-hour tours around the sun."

Dr. J inserted with enthusiasm,

"Before you ask, this isn't something that we were aiming to achieve; we didn't have this one goal in mind. As the events rendered themselves, they seemed purely random. Only by chance where we extracted from those time dimensions, if they are indeed dimensions and returned here.

We have yet to fathom what calendar of events and what theory's seems to apply to our circumstances or if not, we will develop one of our own."

Qwe felt he was starting to warm kindly to everything, his thoughts were sliding into place. Dr. Rym with some supportive facts, started him on a comfortable introduction to their new frontier;

"Most importantly, you must understand that our physical self's are not molecularly altered or changed in any fashion. We are merely sliding into another dimension on a different frequency, then eventually back to where we started."

Dr.J "The world around you is what is changing, not the physical you."

Qwe was solemnly, thoughtfully digesting all that was being offered,

"Let's digress a small bit; you remember in your theory of physics study the ideas put forth, Max Tegmark's four levels, and the six levels of the 'bubble universe.'

Dr. J & I have possibly entered level four or thereabouts. You may recall on that level 'magic' is possible as we were discussing last night.

What Dr. J & I encountered was a very subtle state of the art of magic. What I intend to explain is all we witnessed, and what we experienced was not dramatic or worrisome to life or limb.

Remember; that if people of that time were to witness our cellphone's of today, they would be amazed and call it 'magic."

Dr. J couldn't stand the strain and had to interject again,

"Another aspect that intrigues me especially is the element of Time. My only hypothesis is the entanglement of the crystal to the location and time of the magic folklore. That makes it purely a predictable event which Dr. Rym and I have evidence that makes magic a witnessed fact. Personally, I say that magic is nothing more than spoken mathematics in a lost language.

Now, what we need is logic and analysis and how can we contour the start sequence of transit between worlds. Or in other words, what elements change this earth's frequency that allows us to phase!"

Rym stepping to the whiteboard to illustrate,

"Dr. J & I have undertaken an examination of the crystal, attempting to look at all, if any, information inside the crystal. Utilizing different spectrums of light and varying intensities and color of lazier inquiry. Of course, we are syncing with our mainframes across the way in hopes of a quicker answer.

We hypothesize that the Hadron Collider power surges at the apex of an individual run may be the key. This is an extremity large leap as far as we have found, our phenomena does not alter their tests, and we have no intention to interfere, add to or detract from any one test. Only at that moment, does the crystal absorb the ambient energy sufficiently to activate it.

What also has been discovered, is an alphabet that we humans are unfamiliar with inside the crystals, Dr. J is still running inquiries.

As our phasing transits laid themselves out, the first was a numbing trip; we had concluded we were wherever we were, permanently. We will fill you in with the details at another time."

Rym, still diagraming on the whiteboard,

"So, on the first transit, we focused on surviving."

Qwe had a question,

"What historical period did you arrive in?"

Dr. J "It was a time in the not-so-distant past of our earth as we understand, in what seemed to be Scotland. Our reasoning at that moment was the menfolk were attired in kilts with different tartans. Not a very large leap guessing our location due to fashion, or any thought of historical genus, ha-ha. Just saying that to lighten the mood…sorry, I get over excited on our subject."

(For the reader; That's about as funny as he gets)

"But exactly what period, we could not establish until a subsequent travel event occurred. The second phasing event, we were deposited in the same location, and what appeared to be the same time.

We agreed to travel south for a day and a half and found what we have determined to be Sterling Castle of today, north/west of Edinburgh, Scotland. We chance happened on a fortnight market gathering day on the Castle grounds.

The thought next in mind, after determining our location in time, was our hopeful return home. so, heading back to our phase introduction point, now praying that the test schedule we were counting on would again return us home on that fifth day test at CERN. And so, we were."

Rym, at the whiteboard molding the events for Qwe,
"Dr. J let's bring Qwe up to date with our travel and study ideas."

"A fine idea!"

Rym started in "Our new plans are to go to the location we assume we have already been when we transited, or phased, to get a visual of the lay of the land on foot. With that accomplished we intend… oh yes, I wanted to ask you if interested…"

Qwe "I'm already packed!"

Rym "How would you feel about this Tuesday through Sunday. Dr. J would prefer to stay here and keep at the review all of our data.

We can travel on Eurail, I have excess to a private cabin so I can update you on the way."

Qwe "That sounds fine with me, but Dr., You will understand your daughter, I must inquire first."

Rym "Why don't you head home and pack your things, or at least try to."

Qwe "On my way!"

On his departure, Dr. Rym & Dr. J settled in and started rolling over some different ideas regarding the crystal.

Chapter Four

Dr. Qwe and Dr. Tayas were working in adjacent buildings, it was a clear Swiss late afternoon, so he stopped by her office with a nice idea.

Stepping up to the receptionist, he didn't need to drop names,

"Hi Dr. I haven't seen you in a while…."

Qwe "How is this side of the building holding up?"

"I am getting used to all the construction noise, but the dust sometimes will drive us out! I am goanna request particle masks!"

"Ha-ha, is she in?"

"I'll ck. … yes, she is in the conference room."

"Thanks"

Rounding a corner, he spotted her alone in the glassed room,

"Hello, my wonderful girl,"

Tayas straitening things around the lectern,

"Hi, how are ya… your voice sounds to me as if you are going to ask for something…"

Qwe "If that were true, I would have brought you some flowers!" (kiss)

"Are you done for the day?"

Tayas "Yep! Finished my presentation, seemed to go well, so I am headed home to do laundry."

Qwe "Oh no you're not… I have a very nice Italian restraint to whisk you away too."

Tayas "Hmmm… it's not our second anniversary yet, so I do think you are up to something…"

Qwe "Quite possible …let's go see."

She finished collecting her things, then out into a beautiful Swiss summer nightfall, the distinct outline of the Alps with its backdrop of sky that was beginning to fill in with sparkling stars.

She was familiar with where he planned to go. It was a pleasant short walk, arm in arm without a word to say, enjoying each other's company.

Stepping into a new world of wonderful fragrance, and old-world charm,

Qwe "Un entrambi per due se ti dispiace...

Hostess, "Naturalmente, in questo modo."

Placed into a booth with a relaxed view of the city, Tayas had a thought, this has something to do with what her dad and Dr. J were discussing a couple of nights ago at Tamra's. Qwe tried to start off slow,

"You look very nice after a long day, what's your secret…"

Tayas with a singsong voice,

"Well, hmmm … I don't have one, but I know someone who does… hum?"

With that beautiful inquiring smile that melts butter and her husband,

Qwe, "Ok, so I don't have a poker face,"

Tayas, smoothing the napkin on her lap,

 "Not tonight, but I still love you..."

"What do you think about me tagging along with your dad, and head up to Scotland for four or five days?"

Tayas's smile lit-up again and quickly volunteered, "When do we leave!"

Qwe back peddling a little, "Well, your dad just asked me… but I guess he wouldn't mind if someone else invited themselves along…"

"That's a request he wouldn't deny! I'm his only doting daughter, and he wouldn't even have a second thought about it, Ha!"

Said with a quick confident smile with a certain flair, Qwe, on the other hand, had a questioning look,

"All right, we leave Tuesday on Eurail…Paris first, then on through the Chunnel to London, then north on Britrail."

Tayas, "We haven't had a chance to get away since our honeymoon, oh joy! We can go shopping and a little sightseeing…"

Qwe "You must know this is a field trip concerning work young lady, your plans must pass my senior partners review."

Tayas "You must be kidding, all I have to say is 'daddy please' with a hug and kiss, the rest is history. Let's order dinner then go pack!"

Qwe was pleased to know there was little hope for Tayas not to be included. On the after-dinner walk back to the tube station, with a little more chill in the air, Tayas was still making plans,

"Are we going to any formal engagements or evening at the Play…?"

Qwe "I think you should be lucky with only an outing of shopping dear girl."

Tayas teasingly "Humm…" with a lower lip extended.

Entering their lakeside home, Qwe felt he should call and inform Rym of the inclusion of his daughter.

"Dr. Rym? Qwe here, there has been a ransom placed on our outing."

Rym "I would like to take a wild speculative guess…

Tayas will be in attendance, and if I were a person that takes odds, I would be correct."

Qwe "It seems you should take a chance at the lottery; you will be a winner."

Rym "Actually, I was hoping she might want to."

Qwe "Then we will see each other on Monday. Bonne nuit."

"Bonne nuit Qwe."

Chapter Five

Monday was meet with the four Dr.'s settling on the agenda of the outing; the primary role of the excursion which was to determine the location of the entry/exit phase point. Dr. J was quite pleased that Tayas wanted to come along on the outing, she had been working very hard on projects and he wanted her to do something different.

"Tayas, now take note on our maps of the present and past. The older map is as close as we have guessed to the time we were witness to the surroundings. Keep meticulous notes if you will, locate and note the marker within some geological formation as we have discussed."

Tayas, was thinking on the creditability of this entire enterprise,

"Dr. J, are we assuming too much? How or when or even if it will be possible to 'phase' at will as you say again."

"We think now it is possible to estimate very close to when and how our future transits will occur, I take it you will be traveling on Eurail, so your dad will be able to fill the two of you in on the latest."

The afternoon seemed to fly by! Each of the four doctors exchanging ideas and sharing thoughts of what a tremendous leap into the unknown, this enterprise of discovery will hopefully be...

Dr. J "With no doubt the first step is the most difficult when you understand what is about to happen. In our case, we were just appropriated at the moment with no prior planning.

The fact that your father and I were taken the first and second time and returned safely with no prior knowledge of a plan seems easy to accept. Whoever is next, will possibly have a harder decision to justify the dangers."

That seamed to interest Tayas all the more and wanted to start packing,

"Qwe, let's go home and double check everything. We are taking an early queue' I hope we get to Paris early enough to check on some items I'm in need of."

Qwe, with a knowing smile,

"Hum, you mean to go shopping. You don't need to dress it up as something else."

"Ok shopping, I am all good with that!"

Not so bright, and very early the following morning, the travelers boarded the train,

"Bonjour Doctor pour faire du shopping?
Rym with a chuckle "Why am I not surprised!"

"Hello, my wonderful daughter! You are addressing the new day nicely!"

"Thank you daddy, you are always too kind."

Rym "Well, I do enjoy my job as a dad."
Small kiss by Tayas. Steeping into the rail car,

"Shall we first pick up as we left off yesterday? I know the two of you have more questions, so let's settle in and answer some."

Each stowing some small items of luggage away, while taking-in glances at the sunrise over the Swiss landscape, that would change soon to be the French countryside of the same flavor.

Settling in and comfortably seated, Tayas opened a thermos and asked,

"Cappuccino?"

The pleasant aroma quickly filled the compartment, she passed cups to all, Qwe was quick to start with questions,

"Tayas & I wanted to bring up the issue of 'magic.' How is it you are aware of the individuals that have the ability to-do magic, or charms, if you understand what I am trying to ask?"

Rym "We were unable to find out if everybody is awarded with it, or only existing in limited cases and of what magnitude or power it manifests itself for each individual. We witnessed one individual at Sterling Castle."

Tayas injected "You were at the castle and saw someone use magic?"

Rym accidently hit his cup and spilled a little,

"Woops, shouldn't talk with my hands quite so much."

"Yes, Dr. J & I on the second transfer, we had attired ourselves in a likable costume of the appropriate vintage. We also took along light camping condiment's. On our scouting junket to the south, we came on what we could only assume was Sterling Castle as Dr. J has already told you.

Entering the outer gates, we made our selves blend-in as much possible with the local crofters on what was a market day. Keeping to the fringes of the gathering, it started to rain, so we slipped into a rough looking doorway and found ourselves in a hallway leading down to what appeared to be the food preparation area for the Castle.

We happened on a brusque lady and were addressed roughly in thick Gaelic of the day that we were little familiar with.

She was pointing at our hands and gesturing as if to say, "You carry nothing, go back!"

"With a great waving of her arms indicating up the hallway, not wanting to call attention to ourselves, we exited the way we entered.

Finding our retreat cut off, coming down the hall at that very moment was a cart full of something that took up the width of the passageway, so we made off into another dim hallway that led to a series of chambers. Not knowing where we were going, we decided to return to the first hallway, but there came a sound of someone approaching.

Hiding behind bales of oats, we witnessed as he entered with a wave of his hand, the touches ling the room and hall ignited themselves. Stopping at some opened baskets, he seemed to touch a clay flask or two, levitate and hold them suspended in the air with only one finger.

Sourcing for some other item in a dark corner, he pointed at a torch, it too was levitated onto a close by corbel and inserted itself where the light suited him best.

Finding what he required, gathered his things and proceeded down a different hall. The most amazing thing was, as he entered the hall, all the items he chose, along with a torch, floated after him as he passed on down the hall!

Looking very surprised at each other, scratching our heads, we made our way back out to the market."

Qwe & Tayas were sitting staring at Rym with their mouths slightly ajar,

Tayas "Ok dad, now should I be worried about you spending too much time in that Lab?"
Rym cheerfully,

"My girl, I tell you the truth as I witnessed, please ask Dr. J on your return if you like, he will confer."

Qwe was silently taking all this in stride, logically trying to classify possibilities from his more in-depth background in physics. He didn't find things quite as unusual as Tayas did.

Qwe "Let's finish the story, did you have further troubles leaving the castle?"

"Not at all, and I'm pleased we left when we did, we wanted to return to our introduction points. We have found that five days is a constant, so far Dr. J is now correlating all of our knowns exists and entrances times; also, the peak times when the Hadron Collider is in a hyper state.

He is linking all of our trips to those corresponding events at the Hadron Complex."

Tayas "So, don't you think it was extremely risky to go out the second time, you didn't even tell me."

"Well, I will tell you, the first, was not planned, the second transfer happened as an uncertain idea, meaning we had out costumes, ready in the lab, close to our last exit, entry point. Before the second phase, we had almost put all the pieces in the puzzle regarding the Collider. I intended to tell you about the event, but we were taken before I could bring you into my confidence."

Tayas "What would I do without my father here to answer my every whim! Next time, I want to go."

Qwe "Hold it there, you aren't going anywhere without me...besides, I would be the logical one to go with Rym because I already almost went."

The air was charged about the little conference car with intrigue as it gently rocked on its rails, adding to the overall mystic. The idea, to be part of the past, and be at a functioning Castle, then to be back here and now, with what seemed almost like an easy effort.

Let's not forget to add a heavy touch of adventure, all in attendance seemed riveted!

Rym "We will let all that settle until we get back with Dr. J for now, we should keep this quiet...

Right at that instant, two faces papered themselves on the glass door with big smiles!

Qwe opening the door,

"Hi Oz, Tamra! No gathering would be complete without you both, are you following us?"

Tamra smiling, sliding in next to Tayas,

"We... Well, I overheard your secretary requesting travel plans at the office, hmmm...I didn't overhear them; I made them. You know I'm the big cheese in the accounting/Mtg. dept. all things go through me ha-ha."

Small laughs all around the car, Tayas whispering in Tamra's ear (in regard to the new boyfriend)

"Boy, you work fast!"

Both leaning back as they had their own personal small laugh circle. (For the reader, all of the people present knew each other from the lab, so nobody was new to anybody.)

Tamra started to explain that Ozbetin was from Sterling and thought he would be interested in coming along on her invitation.

Qwe felt he wanted to antagonize her lightly,
"Ah, excuse me, who's invitation?"

Tamra, "Don't worry, we will be going solo when we get to Sterling, Oz has family there…."

Tayas jumped in,
"Maybe you two will be three, maybe you won't, depends on dad & Qwe."

Tamra "Cool, we could all do some shopping around Sterling an stuff."

The men in the car took-on a numb blank look, Oz weakly tried to hold up a semi-smile just for show, but that was easily read through.

Rym "I have no doubt Tamra has our stay over at a nice hotel in Paris, don't forget, it's an early departure as you know, so plan your afternoon accordingly."

Oz "May I say something about shopping? If Tamra & Tayas are heading out this afternoon to do what they do, would you mind if I was to tag along with the men?"

Tamra, with a little nudge and a smile,
"Chicken."

Men laughing,
Qwe "Of course, we can have lunch together and then go our ways."

Rym starting to stand,
"Just right then, I think I'll stretch my legs for a bit, I think we have forty-five minutes until we arrive, sound about right Tamra?"

Checking her watch,

"You are correct Dr."

Not quite in Paris, Qwe & Ozbetin settled in to talk of the Collider, Ozbetin had a very hands-on connection with the physical operation of the Collider as one of the Tech teams on that side of the street.

The girls cheerfully watched the French countryside slide by at a rapid rate and talk about all the good things friends talk about.

Chapter Six

Arriving in Paris on a mild midmorning, hailing taxies, then off to Le Bristol hotel. After a little freshen up in their assigned rooms, the travelers convened in the lobby.

Enquiring of the concierge for a light restaurant for lunch close by, they found themselves off to Bistro Petit.

Each one, especially Tayas, who seemed to take special note of the improvement here and there in the city architecture and atmosphere, mentioning how nice it is to be here again.

All were enjoying a comforting afternoon passing by the men were comfortably scattered amongst the lobby reading various books or newspapers. Noticing the arrival of the girls and amount of cumbersome bundle's, Rym being a good father, gently asked of their intentions.

Tayas "Have no fear dad, we are going to have the concierge mail the big one's home."

Qwe greeted Tayas with a warm smile of understanding, so with all present, the general decision was to dine here at the Hotel.

Tamra took it upon herself to let the men know all about their afternoon in Paris, and her ideas for Sterling. Oz mentioned his sister is looking forward to assisting in any way.

As they were about ready to retire, Rym took Qwe aside to discuss his reconnaissance tour,

"Qwe, I would ask only Tayas and yourself to accompany me on to Alva glen, this should stay amongst the three of us for now,

I would like to have Tayas with us to bring her up to speed if you will, now you have your work cut out for yourself tonight."

Qwe "Hmm… that is truth."

The company bid each other 'Bonne nuit.

A dim misty start to the French day, and all were in good spirits. Stepping outside into the city morning début, the car honks and cigarette flavors in the air, reminded them about other times in this big busy city. Next on up the line, the 'Chunnel,' a stop in London, and change to Britrail, then arriving in Sterling.

Leaving the Queue behind, heading out to the street, Oz was busy looking for his sister in front of the station curbside,

"There, I see her coming up."

Rym, "I'll call a lift for the rest of us."

Oz "No sir, don't bother, I asked her to bring the big car… here she is…Athena!"

A midsized van rolled up, doors opened and quick introductions all around, bags in the boot and off to the family homestead. Athena smiling & telling her brother,

"Hugs and Kisses at home, let's get on…"

Ten minutes later, Oz was enjoying a heartwarming feeling seeing his childhood home again.

As they all entered, Athena explained,

"Mum & Da are on holiday in the Caribbean, Oz told me of your plans, and there is plenty of room here for all. We do have a wonderful family friend; she will see you to your rooms."

Rym "This is unexpected and most kind. I would inquire of an auto rental agency for my travel to Alva glen tomorrow with Qwe and Tayas."

Tayas "What! Athena, Tamra and I had plans!"

Smiling Rym, "I see Qwe that you neglected to sway your wife last night."

Qwe "Well, err…"

Athena "Don't be bothered Dr. we have a car for your use."

Rym "This is very unexpected and very welcome, I usually leave my travel plans in the capable hands of Tamra, I can see she has surpassed herself this time!"

Tamra "Thanks Dr., wanted to change things up a bit, I got to talking with Oz, really he did the rest with Athena's help."

Thank yuzus all-around.

Oz "Well, Samantha, it's been a long couple of months."

"Yes, young sir… You look as if the Swiss climate is still agreeing with you."

Oz "Thank you, Samantha, let me introduce my company, this is Tamra, if you don't mind Tamra's in my room: well, she an' I are...you know..."

Smiles all around and with introductions finished, Samantha set everything else in motion,

"Follow me please; I will show you to your rooms, then please come down to the Family room for Tea at 2:00"

Oz, for his part on the way upstairs, was giving a small tour concerning their home, and twenty or so minutes later, knocking on doors, requested everybody to tea.

On the way downstairs, he let them know a little more about life in Scotland.

"It does get chilly here so don't be bashful, please light the coal, the best way to hedge the chill especially deep in the night.

Yes, and just a reminder, as you know it doesn't get very dark here until about 10:30 or so…"

Rym "This is all so welcoming and thank you again."

All were contentedly enjoying teatime in front of bay windows with, of course, rain on the way, a nice warm fire set the mood perfectly. Tamra had not had the pleasure of Ozbetin's home before, so admiring the artwork and antiques she asked,

"What does your dad do for a living? All this stuff looks kinda rich for someone like you."

Oz "I am very offended! Ha-ha, I am just a lab tech still finding my way, but I did come from not so humble beginnings. Father and Mother taught at the university of Edinburgh and had since retired."

Qwe "I should have put more thought into following that line instead of mucking about in laboratories."

Tayas, "We come along just fine, and are just starting out ourselves."

Rym wanted to get travel plans set for tomorrow so,

"Tayas, I must bring up arraignments for tomorrow, I fear you won't agree when you hear me out, I need to survey sights around 'Alva glen' and a little north, I plan to spend the night at an Inn…"

Tamra interjected, "You will be staying at, Woolpack Inn, located in Tillacutrey for one night —for two…"

Rym "So… you ladies did have a pact! conspiring against me!"

"Well, I need the two of you Tayas & Qwe, the rest can be footloose and fancy-free."

Tamra "I tried Tayas, sorry."

"Well, thanks for the effort."
With a small sigh,

Rym "Fine, that settled, it's about 23 km, two or three hrs. should do it, dress for small hikes and ideas of geological fetchers. I will call the Inn and add a reluctant addition to our group."

Tamra already on her cell, "I got it."

The rainy afternoon lasted into the evening, and at dinner, Qwe was asking Tayas if they had included suitable rain attire.

The answer issued from Tamra,

"You men think that when we girls shop, that it's just for ourselves! Guess what… that's what we were doing in Paris. I know all and what will be suitable for Dr. Rym, Dr. Qwe and Dr. Tayas."

Rym was quite surprised ,

"Tamra you are always a wonder with all of my travel plans, I'll thank you now again once more."

Chapter Seven

All were met with a crisp morning sun and were jokingly asking if it ever went down. Two groups setting off, Athena, Oz & Tamra were off to Sterling Castle, about more tourist business with an inside guide. (Athena was one of the historian at the castle.)

Rym, Tayas and Qwe, set their sights on Alva glen.

"Qwe, would you be so kind to drive? I would like to study the maps."

"Of course, let's stop for petrol and coffee soon."
Tayas "Dad are you sure you need me?"

"Yes daughter, I do, we should have a nice outing, it's been a while for us together on a car trip."

"Your right daddy, we'll enjoy our time."

Stopping here and there to check other glen possibilities along the route, Rym was pouring over maps and rethinking memories,

"Dr. J & I didn't follow this route; this is more to the east of Alva glen or Wood-hill glen, the road comes back west a little farther on."

Qwe "When we get closer, I'm guessing that the countryside will become familiar to you and we'll be able to scout a little on foot, I have the GPS you requested so hopefully it will help make things clear on the map."

So far, the weather had been holding, and Rym wanted to move farther on up the road,

Rym "Our location is in the proximity of Alva glen proper, it's little north, according to our map there is a bridge we must cross over, at that point I think our hike begins."

The lush green expansive valley they were driving through was flanked with smaller individual glens.

Each with an abundance of trees and low shrubs in pleasing harmony with a small stream or 'Burn.'

Coming up on road signs Rym was asking Qwe to bare to the left carry on slowly. Presently, crossing a bridge over Alva burn, he pulled off.

"This all looks mildly familiar, but this is as far as we can go in the car, let's hike a little up the glen."

Setting off on an established path, Rym was explaining the obvious, that all the flora, Broadleaf Maple, Ash, Oak has changed so, it's all older and new to him.

Qwe, "Are we trying to find something or someplace?''
Rym, "Both"

Tayas "What exactly do you mean dad? "

"Well, keeping in line with the crystal, diamonds, rubies, the source of those elements, which are decidedly rarer here in the United Kingdom, only found in single groups and by chance. I think that this crystal of ours has a home. It seems to want to come back, but back to where?''

A way on, Rym wanted a little break, stopping to dig out the map, they all gathered to reconnoiter.

Tayas, "Were the trees dense like it is now, or less."

Rym "There were more trees then, but not as dense as this is now, the Hawthorn bushes are now thicker. This little stream now named Alva burn seemed wider in the past and the level of water was higher.

I did remember a small blueish lake where the glen opened out a little, I don't see any lakes on this new map, but the older map has it noted."

Qwe "Its possible we are just in the wrong glen, I noticed a number of them on the way here, and to the North as well."

Rym "Yes all possible, we haven't gone that far, let's go on a little further, I do remember hiking down a bit first, and back up."

Tayas "Hay you guys, it's starting to get a little darker."
Qwe "We can try our new rain jackets out soon."

"I might have forgotten to bring mine."

Tayas, "No you didn't, I have it in my daypack."

Rym "Daughters are wonderful, thanks"

Moving on only about 500 yds. they seemed to have happened on what appeared to been a very wider part of the stream, stopping to review their surroundings.

Rym "Does it look like on the far side there… A possibility of a very large rockslide?''

Qwe, "It does, let me take some pictures, and while I'm at it, I think I'll put on my rain be gone jacket."

Everybody did likewise, checking the sky and adjusting the fittings.

Qwe" Thank you Tayas, I even have a hood."

Tayas "Everybody does, did you think you were the special one?"

Qwe "That's what you tell me in the dark of the night."

Tayas "Ha hum…. yes, I do, but for now, my dad is the special one because he has mittens included with his."

Rym "So I do, and because of that fact I will never utter another disparagement regarding shopping!"

Tayas," Yeah! Hang on, let's get back to the car, it's starting to come down!"

Getting themselves situated, warming the car, Rym wanted to drive to the north, past Tillacutrey, on to Castle Campbell, which wasn't that far. Slowly taking in visual clues, Rym asked Qwe to stop a few times for pictures from the car due to the rain.

Tayas" Do you remember seeing Campbell castle?"

Rym, "No, only roughly overheard the name, there were times we heard it mentioned in very thick Gaelic of a sort, something like it is used today."

Arriving at the castle, finding it was closed and just as well, rain starting to really come down. Having enough touring for the day, they headed back to the Woolpack Inn.

Rym, "Let's freshen up and meet back in the common room, I want to ask around about earthquakes or any changes through the years."

Tayas & Qwe, later hooked up with Rym, already in conversation with a local Scotts person, the 'bar maiden.'

Rym "Grab a table by the fireplace, I'll be right with the two of you."

Qwe found a perfect one and seating Tayas next to the warmth of the inglenook,

Qwe "Haven't had too much time today to ask how you are feeling?"

Tayas "A little tired, if they have a place here, I would rather dine in, if you don't mind."

Qwe "Sounds good, gives your dad more time to ask around."

Tayas, "Do you think this is all nuts? Has dad carried all this too far?"

Qwe "No I don't think so, I say that because I felt the start of the transfer myself. There has to be more to glean from their experiences as well, and I feel as though it's the tip of the ice burg. I think he is approaching carefully, logically and wow, you should have felt it!"

Tayas's thoughts were wandering, warmed by the fire, the tint of wood burning in the air, speaking absently,

"You know what I'd like?"

Qwe, knowing her look,

"Yes, Chardonnay, be right back."

Qwe walking back with Rym "One for the lady, one for me Dr. has his, so just to fill you in, your girl seems a bit tired and would like to dine in."

Rym "By all means, I think in all my enthusiasm I have come away tired today as well, so enough."

Qwe "Have you found any good information about any geological movement in the neighborhood?"

Rym, "Well yes, sort of, she suggested meeting with an older gentleman who apparently has quite a history here in the town of chasing elements of magic and Alva glen in particular. She gave me his address, if not that, the library tomorrow. She also mentioned they had few major earthquakes Ml 4.7-5.0, years ago, nothing like California, ha-ha, but still, for this local I'll assume that's a lot."

Qwe, "Would you like to try again at Campbell castle, or try the other glen?"

"No to the castle, and yes to another location, I would also like another attempt at Alva glen before it rains. Then maybe the old gentleman, possibly fall back on the library."

Tayas "Tamra was mentioning that Ozbetin is a pilot, maybe an aerial view might help"

Rym "You know, that just might be of great help."
Tayas "Let me give Tamra a call…"

"All right very good."
Qwe, "I asked the barmaid about dining in, she just said,

"Stay where y've landed, I bring along the house menus."

Tayas was still on the phone, Qwe & Rym enjoying the comfortable fire and the rain outside, sat quietly reviewing pictures of the day. Tayas rang off and told Rym that Oz's father owned an airplane and would enjoy taking them on a little tour.

Tayas, "Oz said we are very close and maybe on to the highlands for a side trip if you like."

Rym "That might be very rewarding.''

The next morning had them up early, hiking farther up Alva glen, they came on something memorable,

"There on the opposite side of the rockfall, this small, rounded ridge with sharp rocks lining the top, then down to the stream before that small cave, that appears to be very one I remember."

Qwe, "You have found something or are familiar with the surroundings, yes?"

Rym "I think so Qwe, do you have that map and spade in your daypack?''

Qwe, "I do, I'll grab it."

Moving up a small rise above the cave, rummaging,

"It doesn't look like too much traffic, human or animal passes by, would you think in amongst the top rocks here or down by the cave?"

"I think just down from the top and a step or two on the back side there; last time down around the cave entrance, had some traffic patterns in the grass."

Qwe started measuring it, then digging down to assure the depth, Rym asked to be very careful around the grass at the top to have it appear un-molested when observed again.

While that was taking place, Tayas came up and was marking the GPS quadrant on their new maps.

Tayas "Anything else? How about a picture or two?"

Rym "Yes, and I would like a quick look into the cave again to be sure."

The three moved down the ridge a little, and into the cave.

Rym "Just so. We spent a couple of nights here inside the second cave behind all this collapsed earth, and it was just over there, that was our transit introduction point on the two occasions. Right then, let's be on our way back to town to locate the old gentleman then on to Sterling, I want to relay our findings to Dr. J."

Searching for and easily finding the older gentleman's address, they found no one home. Rym left a card with notes on the back with his number.

Arriving at Ozbetin's a little after tea, Samantha answered their knock at the door and sat them down in the family room, and tea was served once again.

Tamra & Oz and Athena were still out sightseeing, Rym had made his call on the drive back, so all were enjoying the Cole fire and tea.

Watching the rain, mulling ideas around, their conservation drifted,

Tayas "Dad, a thought just struck me, the cave we just visited, was that where Merlin lived?"

Rym "Not too sure at all, let's ask someone who might know."

With that, the front door opened, and in blows Oz & Tamra and Athena. Oz calling out "Anybody around?"

Tayas, "We're in front of the fire come on in, how is the life of a tourist?"

Tamra plopping down exasperated

"Last two days, this castle, or that monument, or you have to see the insides of this or that church, the life of a tourist is overrated."

Athena, the obvious choice for historical information, was off in the kitchen (Samantha, born & raised and was the housekeeper, treated like family)

"Samantha, could you help fill in the blanks?"

"Sure, as I can, as much as Athena is the real expert. For what I know, I very much enjoy wee treks on the glen with all the small waterfalls. The wee cave you are thinking of; it's called 'Smugglers cave' I duny know anything about that, but it has a rumor that Merlin and the 'Lady of the Lake' stayed there often. The bones of a dwarf were found hundreds of years ago, and the person that found them died a fortnight after, whether tizz true or not, I rather like the folklore."

Athena just stepping back in overhearing some of the conversations,

"Their use to be a little bigger lake adjacent to the Cave and the water had a blue shade, folklore says it was that color because the Faeries would always bathe in that lake!

And yes, to what Sam was mentioning about Merlin, that's the rumor."

Tayas "Well dad was telling us….

-- Rym braking in, "We were just at the cave but hadn't a torch."

Sam "Oh it doesn't go on far, it has collected a lot of earth, cave-ins I am told."

"Well, that's your answer Tayas, we might have been walking in the very footsteps of Merlin!"

Sam "Out of old gray, be right back."

Rym leaning into Tayas,

"Sorry dear. I thought you were going to slip and say that I spent the night there."

Sam stepping in with a tray "Tea rather of ya?"

Tamra "I am going to be rude and skip that, how 's a glass of rich red wine, the fire with rain on the outside and my favorite peps inside! Anybody else, I know it's only 4:00…"

Oz, "I'm in."

And around the rooms it went.

The next morning, Oz was collecting his flight case, keys, and asking the room who would like to go flying. Tamra, Tayas, Athena and Sam all wanted to do lady things (shopping), so the men were off to the not so blue sky. On the way, Oz was letting them know he was instrument rated, so weather was not a problem. IFR plan submitted, ready to go Qwe was admiring the twin 421 Cessna while Oz was doing the walk-a-round inspection of the airplane.

"I wasn't aware you flew."

Oz, "I only do up here, it costs a lot, I come up every couple of months to stay current, mostly to see Mum and Dad."

Qwe, "This is very kind, I hope this won't take too long so you can get back to Tamra. I know her story, she won't be happy if I keep you too long."

Oz "I am not worried I can handle her."

Both Qwe and Rym started laughing

"Keep that thought…"

All of a sudden, Oz had a worried look,

Qwe "If she wants it, she gets it!"

Small laughs all around.

Walk-a-round and preflight checks complete, radio weather, to ground then hand-off to the tower, holding for some incoming traffic a few moments, then on to the active rwy. The twin easily got up to speed and rotated into the air. The pilot and passengers had headphones with a microphone boom, makes it a lot easier to hear & talk to each other.

Oz informing the others,

"It's only about 7 min. away there is a 1000 Ft. min. and it's somewhat steep, so I'll approach from the top of the valley as slow as I can, we can sort of make lazy S's to slow down a little more.''

Rym "Qwe can you take some photos; I know we didn't bring the right camera but give it a go."

And so, gently floating down the glen with the power back, then another pass around again on a wingtip, to get the wing out of the way of the picture.

Oz, "That's Campbell castle, I like this rout on to the highlands for a quick overfly."

Rym "Oz I don't know if you can, but is Perth and Dundee just came to mind is that possible to find?"

Oz, "No sweat, we are heading north, north, west, then we will turn to the East then southeast then south to home, it's one of my favorite routes."

Rym "Dundee was another stop of Merlin's and may in the future be useful."

The over flight and all the sights were met with very grateful thanks and help slipping the airplane back in the hanger, they were back at the house before they knew it.

They were greeted with a note suggesting a 12:30 lunch spot if back they were back in time, so next stop was 'Hermann's' a Scottish-Austrian favorite of Sam's.

With all things for the day done, time to ready the travelers for their trip back to Geneva. Tayas and Tamra wanted to stop again in Paris for a short time, so true to form, they did.

Chapter Eight

Monday morning came early for all except Dr. J, he had been up most of the night.

"Well-well come along, let me show you what I had put together, thanks to Ozbetin before you left, he gave me a history of past and future plans of times and dates for the collider so that we can plan accordingly."

Dr. J apprising the two travelers strangely,
"You look as if a coffee or two would be in order…"

Qwe "Thank you, that's what we forgot, I'll be right back!"

Rym meanwhile was showing Dr. J his pictures and aerial video, and the two agreed on the location.

Next was their question on who would phase next time, Dr. J being older was hoping that Rym would agree that Qwe would go.

Rym "Absolutely of course, but I am worried that Tayas will force her will also to accompany me."

Qwe just returning from the cafeteria with the wake-up juice passing to all who wanted, voicing a concerned thought,

"I have been thinking all along, who would be next to transit"

The two Dr's glanced at each other, Rym stepped up,

"We were just thinking that very thing and…"
Qwe, "Is there a way we can shorten the stay."

Dr. J "Possibly, according to the test dates for the Collider, there are three dates closer together, but that is not a given that on that transit, or your return will be any sooner, it still may require the six days, we don't know what will be possible yet."

Qwe, "I would like to be considered to be one of the groups to go. I know what it starts to feel like, you two are going to have to work that out between the two of you."

Rym "Already done, welcome phase partner!"
Qwe slapping his hands together and rubbing,

"When do we go!"

Dr. J "Hold on to your keyboard! We have a lot to plan,
most of all, Rym has reminded me about your lovely wife, and what
contingents we must plan for in that event."

Qwe "I know this is going to be a tuff sell."

And so, the plans of the Dr.'s carried on through the rest of
the day.

Tayas, back home from work was unpacking the things
they bought in Paris and light heartedly humming as Qwe came
through the house,

Qwe "Well, how did you fair on your Monday back at it?"

Tayas "I am going with you,"

Still humming not skipping a beat, folding things, turning to
him, with a look that all of a sudden would melt rocks,

"I will not stand by and lose you to Time, I love you. You
will not go without me."

Qwe standing transfixed, decided to slide around the matter,

"That's wonderful I was having…"

Tayas "That didn't work, I know you too well… I am
going!"

This was one of the two or three times he had ever
encountered her this way; he still wanted for some reason to try and
explain it away,

"I was goi…"

Tayas "Remember your poker face? It's not on. I am
going."

With that flatly presented, Qwe set his mind on his work
partners, and their rebuttals…well, tomorrow.

The next morning, entering the office together Tayas &
Qwe presented the new agenda (according to Tayas) to Dr. J & Dr.

Rym. Needless to say, it was a long morning, all though Tayas did ultimately win out, the settled-on travelers were Qwe & Tayas.

The option of a third was not intended at this time. This was meant to be a discovery junket, hopefully short and to establish that in fact it was this earth we are now on, that the phasing have been to and from.

The rest of the day was left to plan when and what was to be included in the event of an extended stay. Tayas was aware of the camp-like conditions; being a person of the outdoors in younger years with her dad Rym, was not in any way a deterrence. Each had very seriously studied the reality of their undertaking, it was meet with a very empirical approach with all the facts they had at hand, and with a lot more wonders.

Departure time was in two days, so necessary items of period clothing, and lite overnight necessities and dried foodstuffs.

Camera, flashlight, lighter must be made to blend in with their phasing costumes. They would travel in their Street clothes in case the destination was at another time.

(For the reader: Their offices and laboratory were on opposite sides of the street, the test Lab being underground within the circle of the 27 Km Hadron Collider.)

Upon the appointed time the travelers were presenting themselves as collected and calm as possible, given that they are about to go to who knows where and for how long?

Dr. J was busying himself with the crystal and Dr. Rym was monitoring the test start at the Collider

Dr. J "Now remember that you have the first chance to return in 4hrs., then another in 8hrs. Stay close to the cave after you check on the location and place the marker which is 100 yds. up the ridge. If you do not return on their second test, you have 4 hrs more to wait.

You hopefully will not interact with anybody.

We didn't see anyone in Alva glen when we were there. I know there is plenty of water in the glen and a cave to wait in if rain is present. Tayas, this is very courageous of you."

Tayas "He's not going anywhere without me. If it means other worlds, so be it."

Rym "I have all the confidence you both will be right back. We are within ten minutes if they are on schedule. As far as we have learned, stand within a radius of about 15ft. of the crystal it will start to modulate a very pleasing sound, we will make a video record of it this time since we will be here instead of in the phase medium.

You have your shabby backpacks, oh, Qwe if you are on a different earth, be so kind as to bring back geologic samples. I know we discussed all this, and I'm talking in circles."

Rym trying to be stoic "Tayas, I want to see my favorite smile in a couple of hours…"

Dr. J "It is starting. Watch the display Dr.''

Tayas, "I'll be right back dad! Wow, that does sound different! I like it……."

Chapter Nine

His focus of the two started to take on a fuzzy TV look and linger…. Tayas had Qwe's hand, both looking at each other, then slowly dimming.

Their next prompt, the dimming started to become slowly light, out of focus lingering then clearly standing on solid ground, instantly knowing it was Alva glen on a beautiful sunny day.

Starring at each other in semi-shock, slowly adjusting to the new fragrance and temperature of their surroundings. Yes, the cave was different from where they stood, it didn't appear collapsed on the interior.

Yes, the lake was broader, and it had a light blue tint that wasn't there when they were here last. It really did look wider, and the evidence of the rockslide was not present on the far side of the lake.

Tayas "Wow, Wow…this...Wow, I um…"
Qwe astounded, taking in as much as he could, absently,

"You're starting to sound like Tamra."

The two nervously laughing, then appraising each other, checking to see if all their parts were back where they should be after the transit.

Qwe, "Do you recall the lake, or at the time we were here, it wasn't as large as it is now, and now it's light blue."

Tayas, "Remember, Athena and Samantha told us some folk stories about Alva glen and the lake is light blue because the local Fairies used the Lake to bath in…fun!"

Qwe "Wow, I remember… now I sound like Tamra!"
Tayas "I want to jump in!"

"Ok, earth to Tayas come in Tayas… let's hike up to set a location for the marker and take care of our checklist first."

Tayas "OK, but which earth!"
Qwe "Excellent point!" as he hiked off.

Sort a mumbling to herself, following

"I still want to jump in…"

The travelers followed the rocky ridge to the top, then a little down the backside, a measured distance paced out foot by foot.

Tayas amused herself with taking pictures, videos, while Qwe stopped, took out his photos from the first trip, lining up the photo with the rock ridge, was sure he was on the correct spot. All right, digging down about 18" and inserting the round hand size sample of polished turquoise.

(It was decided that turquoise was inconsistent with the surrounding Metamorphic rock and make it obviously easier to establish a clear identification.) Carefully restoring the area to be as undisturbed as possible. With that done the two headed back down to the cave mouth.

Qwe," Well we have 3hrs. left maybe, so let's check out the cave, see how far back it goes."

Tayas "Hay you know, I don't care to be underground a lot. I'll stay out here take some pictures and get our salami & cheese lunch ready and I'll grab some water first. Yeah, I think I'll stay out here."

(Her true thought was of a little mischief,)

Qwe "Ok, but I need to take the camera in case it gets interesting, if it does get bigger or go deeper, I'll stop."

Tayas "All right, do you think we should change clothes?"

Qwe "I will when I get back, but that's probably a good idea."

Qwe turned and headed into the cave with the flashlight, Tayas turned and headed over to the lake for some water.

It was a perfect day, warm not too hot no wind, with few clouds. Standing on the lake shore it didn't look as blue right next to it, she tasted the water and was very sweet.

Thinking to keep to her plan, she decided to jump in, it would be fun to say I swam with the fairies.

Venturing a test toe touching the small lake of course was very cold, so she dropped her things, and was going to change anyway.

One two three… jump splash and in! It was only 5 feet deep, she had to catch her breath, the surrounding water started to quickly feel warmer, smoothing her hair, submerging all the way scratching her head.

Among the bubbles at first, she thought she heard her name! Surfacing she looked around the shore and… nobody, well just the shock of the water maybe. She didn't notice at first, but the water was getting pleasant, she went under again and just held her breath.

"Tayas, welcome"
She surfaced again! What was it, who was it…speaking,

"Yes, what or who is it?"

No response above water so back under, the water was now comfortably warm.

"I am called 'Lady of the Lake' do not be fearful, I have been waiting for you."

Tayas "I am just thinking, I'm not talking underwater, … and you can hear me?"

"Yes"

Tayas "I must get air" surfacing grabbing a big gulp, under again…

"Tayas, if you can relax when I am here, you will have no need to surface, try to calm yourself."

"Really, I umm I'll try, wait! one more breath, (up, down)
Tayas "Are you there?"
In a relaxed, comforting voice

"Yes…now, calm yourself…. concentrate on my voice."
"Ok, I'll try."

Tayas opened her eyes, this time underwater her vision was clear, beginning to take form in front of her was a shimmering opaque beautiful woman, seemingly floating on a very lite breath of air caressing her hair, and dress to swirl occasionally slightly, and a smile that rivaled her own.

"Let me tell you about myself, I am what you would simply call a good fairy or wise mage. I have been expecting a traveler, let us not concern ourselves with explanations now, we are in need of you in the other worlds to assist us. All it requires is your presents."

Tayas "I am at a loss; I have no special gifts to offer, and what do I call you?"

"I am called Nyneve, when you leave my water world, you will be reminded, without your knowing of some low gifts you already have, you will carry them into your world to help.

You may not understand who you are helping or enhancing, they will in turn, recognize and thank you. Your gifts will not interfere with anything you don't want them to."

Tayas "I am very grateful, I think…I hope I am not rude in any way; I am very… overwhelmed?"

"I will give you calming charm now, Qwe is coming and is afraid you are drowning, I will not talk with him as yet. Thank you Teases Feuch."

"That's my birth name how did you find that: few people know it."

Lady of the Lake softly fading "Yes, He is here…"

Qwe quickly noticed that the cave had a lot more depth than the last visit. The main cave branched off once into a slightly smaller 'room,' once there he noticed another in the dim light. Naturally feeling inclined to investigate farther. He noticed evidence of some small fires and bones of what looked like rabbit, finding the 'hallway' starting to narrow a bit. Having to bend over so to make his way farther in.

Finding what looked like grass mats here and there, another fire circle. Continuing on, the cave narrowed again moving through on to another 'room,' his light was picking up a rainbow-like reflection. Qwe then happened on a papyrus paged book sitting on a rock shelf, it was full of runes he was not familiar with. Deciding he should get a few pictures, he carefully turned the weathered pages, photographing 5 or 6. Some different reflections from his light, now more profound in the dark cave system almost caught his fancy to go deeper to investigate the reflecting colors, then thinking of Tayas, he retraced his steps.

Reaching the cave mouth, he didn't find Tayas anywhere, starting to worry a little, walking towards the lake with no sighting of her standing. Walking on closer he saw her! She was just hovering underwater! Dropping his pack and launching himself, grabbing her pulling her up!

"Tayas!"

Tayas in a wonder "What!"

Qwe then looking at her, she had the most beautiful calm smile,

"Why... what happened?"

In a calm voice, with water running off everywhere.

"I'm fine, really."

"I thought you were drowning!"

Both coming up out of the water,

"No, I wasn't. I was talking to the 'Lady of the Lake."

Qwe "Did you hit your head on something falling in, what happened!"

Tayas calmly walked to the shore and started putting on her costume,

"I wanted to get some water, and it tasted so good, so I decided to jump in."

Qwe "But you weren't moving and its sorta...warm..."

Tayas "I told you I wanted to swim in the Fairy Lake, so I did. When I put my head underwater, I clearly heard my name."

Qwe "Hang on, you are confusing me."

Tayas, slipping on the traveling costume, tucking in her tattered clothes and putting on hide sandals.

Tayas "You should do the same, I am fine don't worry about me really, I'll tell you all of it. How about we grab some water and head for the cave."

Qwe, shaking his head, wondering what happened, changing his clothes and filling their clay pot with water, heading back to the cave,

Qwe "You wear wet well."

Tayas "Rather dashing yourself, halfway wet."

Qwe, "Why are you so calm, this isn't your normal reaction to situations, you tend to be more animated."

Tayas was striating her hair, while Qwe was getting lunch things out.

"The Lady of the Lake gave me calming thoughts, along with breathing under water."

Qwe "What! wait, what…"

Tayas "Maybe I should jump back in and ask for the same for you I am fine, really, taste the water, it's terrific."

Qwe "Would you please explain…"

"Ok, I jumped in, and while my head was underwater, I heard my name. I shot up thinking it was you, but no, so I wanted to straighten my hair, so I went under again. Then she introduced herself as 'The Lady of the Lake' and told me that I could stay underwater with her as long as she was with me. She was explaining that I was to help them, guess she meant the fairies, she gave me a gift of low magic and that I was to take it back to our world. There, that's all of it. I would help who, I don't know, hum, well, she didn't actually call it magic, 'gifts' was how she put it. Could you hand me a bite of jerky please."

Tayas absently pointing at a package by Qwe, levitated it and slowly moved towards her.

Really goes without saying that their mouth's draped open. Tayas dropped everything, jumped up and ran around to the back of Qwe with her hands on his shoulders, the bag still slowly fowling Tayas until it came within reach where she plucked-up her courage to timidly snatch it out of mid-air.

Qwe with a very astonished look,

"I will safely say, we can call it magic!"

Tayas sitting was holding her fingers in her lap,

"I think the calm charm has worn off! what, how, what!"

Qwe standing now was staring at Tayas

"Maybe we should both jump in the lake! Time for some calm."

Tayas was thinking of how she was going to not appear different when they do get back.

"Ok, maybe I should practice a little, I have it, so I better get used to it."

Pointing at the water pot, nothing happened. She thought for a second that the first event was by chance.

Qwe noticed her quandary,

"Do you want the pot?"

"Yes."

Up and over it slowly hovered into her waiting hand. As soon as she touched it, it settled comfortably in her grasp.

"So, you must concentrate on the object, point, and it's yours, with one finger, maybe. This could be troubling, but I guess I'll live with it.

Let's get some lunch down, we have one more hour to go. Maybe you can get some practice, and I forgot to ask, how are you feeling?"

Tayas "Fine, ok, fine yes I am all right fine I think, excuse me while I help myself to a biscuit."

Pointing, it came slowly towards her, now lightly laughing with a very pleased with herself smile, she plucked it out of the air.

Qwe "Showoff, this is going to be harder to live with than I thought, maybe."

Qwe, after lunch, asked if she could do the dishes with no hands, and she busied herself doing just that. Remarking to herself,

"This just might work out after all!"

At the appointed departure time both didn't know what to expect, so standing hand in hand looking into each other's eyes with hopeful anticipation.

The whimsical vibrating high harmony sound also contained a small slow buoyant vibration, slowly out of focus then back in focus as it happened before.

Dr. J and Rym in the Lab patiently waiting very hopefully, then very gratefully hugging Tayas after a prudent few moments.

Rym "You made it! How was the trip?"

Qwe perceptively looking at Tayas

"Do you want to tell them or shall I."

Tayas had a look of pure mischief in her eyes,

"Watch this dad!"

She focused on a coffee cup across the room… and you know the rest, right into her fingers, and two more mouths had draped open!

Rym," Qwe, do you also have the ability?"

"No, the Lady of the lake didn't pass that on to me, just look at that smile on Tayas thou!"

All were standing back admiring Tayas, her new trick was truly amazing.

Dr. Rym & Dr. J began asking questions from every angle, but Qwe insisted on Tayas sitting down, with a serious face he jokingly told her,

"Tayas, I think you are turning blue…"

Tayas with a quick deep intake of air and a concerned look, quickly putting hands on her cheeks,

"Really?"

Qwe with a loving smile,

"No, just happy we are all safe."

She lovingly pushed him away.

Rym was a little tired of being out in the cold

"The full story please."

Chapter Ten

Questions were answered, each one present had the answers they needed, Rym and Qwe wasted no time making plans to go back to Alva glen and check for the marker.

The next small trip would be an incredibly significant piece of affirming evidence. This would, in fact, establish the presence of a single earth, or with physical evidence not in place, prove the multiple earths theory. Each one in the group was very aware of the world changing significance if, in fact, the marker was not present here and now.

Dr. J was especially in a good rush to get that checked on, so Qwe & Tayas volunteered to fly up to sterling on Monday.

Giving the weekend for each of them to put some perspective on the events of the week. Tayas spent her time on fine-tuning her newly acquired skill, wondered if anything other than levitation was on the list she might be gifted with. Not knowing where to start, nothing else became very apparent as of it yet… Qwe was deep in thought about the significance of everything and what real help were they, or could they be?"

A sunny Monday found the two at the Geneva airport early. Tamra and Oz dropped them off with a reminder that Athena would pick them up at the Edinburgh airport and they would again be her guests. A quick, uneventful flight found them bouncing along with Athena in the family car and were in Sterling before they knew it.

The two were enjoying the Scottish countryside once more, and soon Oz and Athena's warm family home.

Athena "You two know how everything works, Sam will see you to your room, then pop down for Tea."

Tayas was almost embarrassed about all the hospitality,

"We had no intention of putting you through all this for a second time, but we are, very very grateful."

Athena "Well Tamra was telling Oz and really it was their idea, also I want to add in a request. I like to keep up with places and close by landmarks involved with history. I was wondering if I might tag along on your small trek tomorrow?"

Qwe "Absolutely fine! The company is always welcome, I'm sure you can possibly update us historically as well."

Athena "I might add, I would like to include our driver, he and I like the walk."

Tayas "Now I have a question for you, are we intruding on your personal time?"

Athena "Absolutely not. We as well like the company; you will find him a lot more than a driver."

———————————————

The early morning was meet with few clouds and a new Jaguar sedan. Athena introduced Artemis as a very close friend, kindly invited Qwe to the front seat. Athena had everything else planned.

At Alva glen, with rain jackets and cameras, started off on the now well-defined trail following it deeper into the glen.

Artemis, a Botanist, now walked into the role of a naturalist, pointing out Ash, Broadleaf Maple and Hawthorne among other varieties. All had sparking leaves from the overnight rain, now with the morning sun giving everything a fresh feeling of newness.

The hike outwardly welcomed them along, the waterfalls were lightly trickling, babbling and dancing, an enjoyable sound adding to the feel of the little adventure. Qwe in the lead with thoughts of the last time they phased and taking notes as to the physical position of things.

Tayas and Athena were taking pictures, with an artsy flair or so they thought, and having a nice time at it.

They met up by the cave, Tayas was standing off by the lake and had a look of quiet disappointment.

Qwe came up,

"It's not as blue anymore, wonder if the 'Lady' is still here."

Qwe "Didn't she say, I am present in water?"

Athena refreshingly had all the research in folklore at her fingertips and knew all about it.

"According to legend, she is present in all lakes, and small bodies of water, just not at the same time. It's kinda like 'Entanglement' you guys remember from physics, she has an association with water and is able to appear in one body of water, then across the universe in another! "

Qwe "Yes, and it's still a mystery to us in the Physics department."

Tayas "I know Tamra and Oz have told you both about magic and my gifts, but again this cannot go farther, please understand."

"It's an honor just to be present to see this, and yes it will be a secret we'll use much temperance with."

Tayas "I wanta put my hands in to see if I can feel her presence."

Moving off to the shore and submerging hands, her expression went blank,

"Welcome Tayas, I am weak here, this will be explained to you in the future, you do not need to look for the stone, it is on my World, not this one."

Tayas "Hello Ma' Lady! I am glad to be with you again, I have so many questions."

"Yes, they will be answered in time. We are making ready for a vast confrontation and will count on your family heavily. I must go, you will do well, I will talk through someone in the future, questions will be answered."

Qwe "Well? Is she here?"

Tayas "Yes, she told me the stone was not here, its back on her world! We not only traveled through time but landed on an entirely different earth!"

Qwe froze "Schrodinger Equation & Drake Equation: possibilities of multiple Earths and complex life! We can now insert those probabilities that the equation needed! This one is really going to change every-thing!

All of what we know! Ok, ok all right… I gotta check on the marker, ok, come on let's check the cave first."

Qwe excitedly dug out the light, and they all entered, coming to what was the first room, the hallway had collapsed covering the access to the other places. Here and there had evidence again of campfires but no other refuse.

Athena "How was it laid out in the past?"

Qwe "Well, there were three different rooms with small archways connecting them."

Qwe wasn't surprised with the collapse, also mentioning to Tayas,

"I still want to go check the marker; I hope that doesn't offend your 'Lady Nyneve' too much."

Tayas "Let's go!"

Hiking up to the rock ridge again, then once again addressing their pictures for reference.

Qwe started digging, where he could, Tayas still taking more pictures, was interrupted by,

Qwe "Nothing in the first hole, I'll dig to the right and left of the first location."

Everybody else had found some flat rocks for sitting and started setting out their lunch items, Qwe joined them and informed them that,

"The 'Lady' was right! We were in another world and another time! How are we going to present this to the Physics community!"

In a very calm voice with salami and cheese in hand, Tayas off handedly volunteered,

"I think I am getting rather fond of Alva glen in this World and in a different one, do you really think that Merlin and Nyneve would stay here or there I mean? I guess I can ask her next time."

Qwe "I can't believe it! You with all the questions all the time why aren't questioning this?"

Tayas "Well, if you recall, we just got back from here that wasn't here. It was a copy, or this world is a copy of the other, either way, you and I have walked on both, and I, let me underline, I have the gift of magic on both, and we can never tell anybody! Kinda sucks."

Qwe "Ha-ha…Tayas you are so excepting without all your usual questions, I suppose I should also be since you are right, we have landed on both, and you do have a touch. Not only magic…"

Qwe gave her a smile.

Tayas "Well what do you think, we found Merlin and the Lady of the Lake in another likable world?"

Qwe "Now this brings up the question of running into yourself. A grand Physics paradox we are now part of if I see myself on an alternate earth.

Do we cancel-out our existence altogether, or just on that earth? Or does one cancel out the other and the original stay whole? Which one is the original? Is it impossible to do anything to my other self to change my history, or does naught happen? If we decide to go have a drink together, do we even bother to talk about old or new times since we are me. Myself & me could be very boring!!"

Tayas "I haven't ever given that much consideration, being that it was an impossibility in the past, but now we are thrust into it, and must treat it as a real possibility."

Qwe "Well, I offer up silence for the moment…Still thinking, but how is magic's source only on one earth…. Ok, I will leave that one until later … Sorry, I interrupted you, the question was about Merlin and the possibility of…"

Athena "I give in, this is all too exciting! From all my research, Merlin's time was possibly 40 years before Arthur. Merlin apparently had visions of the future and was able to materialize in Arthur's time. If that is true, then he may have been the first-Time traveler. There are a lot of different interpterion's of his whereabouts. Some historians hold that Merlin is laid to rest in Rennes Britney, France. Newer investigations have his resting place in Marlborough Mound, Bath Scotland, my guess would be closer to Bath. And yes, this is where he and the Lady of the Lake are suspected in staying. "

Tayas, "If I forget, remind me to look into all that when we get back, I will need your help."

Athena "Love to help in any way!"
Qwe "Thinking of that, does your magic still work here?"

With a thought, Tayas pointed at her water cup and sent it to Athena and back.

"I still have the touch!"

It was the first time that the other two had witnessed her gift and they were speechless!

Qwe, wanting to head back to Athena's house before too late, suggested they head back to the car.

Tayas, "I feel like I am rude not saying goodbye to the 'Lady of the lake' so until next time, Bon par."

Tayas gave a small wave goodbye, and down the trail they went.

Chapter Eleven

Wednesday was meet with more inquiries by all, the extraordinary announcement of traveling to a different earth was of course, answered with even more questions. Dr. J & Dr. Rym thought they had settled on a theory, with all this new information, now everything would change.

Who, if anybody could, or should they share this new-found wealth with? It had been unanimously agreed that Taya's talents would not be unveiled to anyone other than this intimate group.

The overriding issue focused on the paradox of meeting oneself. Discussions ranged all around the circle of Dr.'s, and still, with no design of any suitable answer was presented.

After their lengthy discussions of the day, Qwe asked Tayas to dinner at the Italian restraint, and she gratefully excepted with a tired small smile.

While in the elevator with other people from the complex, Tayas noticed a man trying to slip a purse out of a ladies oversized handbag and tried stashing it in his pocket. Without really thinking Tayas pointed at it and closing her fingers, it fell to the floor. The man couldn't bend over due to the crowd, he didn't try to retrieve it.

Excusing himself at the next floor, Tayas pointed and retrieved the object without any notice. The lady in question exited on the same level as Tayas & Qwe.

Tayas asked Qwe to wait for a second,
"Excuse me, may I bother you just one minute?"

"Yes?"

"My name is Dr. Tayas, I noticed a man in the elevator take this out of your bag, I was able to retrieve it from the floor."

The lady did not understand at the moment...
"Excuse me?" Looking a little confused,

Tamra "This is yours, yes?"

The lady looking at the purse, then in her bag,

"O, my lord…Yes, that is mine! How… what happened?"

"I noticed A man reached into your bag and take that out."

"How were you able to get them from the man?"

"Well, just lucky I suppose."

"Yes, sorry, my name is Dr. Mera, what was your name again?"

"Dr. Tayas, I thought that was a terrible thing to do, hope it helps."

Mera was looking closely at Tayas, then her aura, and seemed to come to an understanding with herself, coming closer to Tayas she said

"You are gifted, thank you for your help. We will talk again."

Tayas seemed a little surprised, Qwe coming up

"Everything ok?"

Tayas "Yes, yes let's go."

Mera, "I won't forget, thank you."

Seated comfortably at the restraint Tayas gave Qwe all the needed details,

"Mera seemed to know about me, gifts and something in the way she looked at me."

Qwe supportively "You must try to be unnoticed in public, nobody would remotely understand."

Tayas, "I know I will, really didn't think, it kinda just happened, kinda fun actually."

Chapter Twelve

The CERN responsibilities always were foremost and had all the Dr's attention for the week, it seemed to be a pleasant distraction.   Everybody was settling back into their regular responsibilities and habits.

They fell back into lunching together at the cafeteria quietly discussing the impact of all this would have on the physics world. Individual ideas on future longer trips, and of course, the dilemma of meeting oneself was always high on their list.

On one of these occasions, Dr. Mera noticed Tayas among the group and came over to asked if she would briefly stop by her office after lunch.

Tayas was interested in what she may have to offer, taking the elevator to Dr. Mera's floor, after greeting the receptionist, she was directed into Dr. Mera's office.

"Welcome Tayas, I wanted to thank you again, and approach something we may have in common."

Closing her office door behind them, directing Tayas to a seat, standing beside her desk she pointed at her pen, and it floated slowly towards Tayas. Understanding immediately, she was in good company, smiling,

Tayas "It seems we do have something in common, how did you know?"

"I was born with the gift and can sense it in others. You probably have questions, and I will be happy to answer, but first, would you tell me how you came upon your gift?"

This put Tayas in a defensive position, not wanting to talk about the phasing part.

"I am not sure how much to volunteer, but it was a gift from the 'Lady of the lake.'"

Mera, "Was she strong, was it somewhere here in Switzerland, sometimes at a distance, she can be weak."

"It was in Scotland, north of Sterling along Alva glen.''

"Astounding! I will speak candidly, you have found one of the crystals, and you have convoked a way to travel!"

Tayas was amazed but still wasn't sure, hesitating,

"Hum, I think I should talk with my group and…"

"Have no concerns, I am from that world."

Tayas was shocked,

"You are? How then are you then in this position here at CERN?"

Dr. Mera "I came from a later time than when you were there, but I was sent back to the time you just may have come from due to my Gifts to help."

Feeling much more at ease, Tayas poured her story out, along with a lot of questions, which in turn some were answered.

Mera "I would like to meet your group if they would agree?"

Tayas "I will bring the matter to their attention and let you know, thank you so very much, this has helped me personally quite a lot."

When Tayas got back to the Lab, Tamra was there asking for her.

Athena, Ozbetin's sister, had been doing some more research. (Remember she is one of the historians at Sterling Castle).

Since Tayas was inquiring about folklore when she was staying with her in Sterling, she had found some entries into some ancient parchment regarding Ambrosius (Merlin).

Tamra "She e-mailed what she found to Oz, and he gave the note to me, she said you two forgot to exchange e-mails."

At that moment Tayas was debating with herself whether or not to tell Tamra all about what was going on, but held her thoughts for now.

Back at home, Tayas needing help sorting out all the new information, Qwe was just as mystified. Dr. Mera had laid a foundation that gave both of them a totally new direction.

"She had said she has heard of me and, knew my full birth name--

'Feuch triose taidhri'Chean' (older Scottish Gaelic)

"Yours, Qwerty Rtyuiop, don't ask me to correctly pronounce either one, I wrote them down with some other notes. She wants us to get together and mentioned we will be shocked and overjoyed!"

So, they sorted through what they had into the night. Tayas thought it would be difficult to introduce an outsider, but to her surprises, Dr. J & Dr. Rym welcomed the idea. So, it was set for the next day, a private lunch.

(For the reader: without dragging you through all the repetitive dialog, I'll jump to the good stuff)

Dr. Mera with all the information presented, had thought she would save the best for last. She silenced the gathering and had one more thing that needed to be said, she took her time starting to lay it all out, then,

"Qwe & Tayas... you are the parents of three princesses, one is here on this earth. Her name is Tamra, the two others are named Lyka and Carisa."

Taya's appearance was one of hopeful believing and impossibly understanding.

Tayas after a few moments of consideration, excitedly

"Wait a while, the Tamra I know! The one I was raised with here in Geneva, the one I talk to every other day?"

Mera "Yes, that very one. Qwe, yourself and your family are from that time, the same one the two of you just returned from, we cannot explain the slight age variation now, but they were birthed when you both were 17 years of age.

Now the difference between Tamra and yourself is only 3 years. We don't have an explanation yet. My group is trying to deal with an avalanche of new information, Qwe & you Tayas were also born with the gifts you recently reacquired, Qwe, you will be reacquainted with yours when you are with the Lady next time.'"

At this point, Mera let them alone to digest everything she had said,

Tayas in very much shock, looking at Qwe with a small gulp,

"Hi…Dad?"

Qwe volunteered his best

"Hi… Mom??"

The room was plunged into silence.

Chapter Thirteen

Qwe and Tayas had the weekend coming up and wanted to invite Tamra over for dinner. The two had decided they would introduce themselves to their new-found daughter???

The new mom & dad had resigned themselves to the fact that it was unavoidable with upcoming transit plans in the works.

Tamra, always assuming much arriving with Ozbetin. With smiles and wine in hand, she dove past everybody straight into the kitchen, rummaging through a drawer on a search for the corkscrew.

Opening the bottle with much flare, grabbing four glasses and back in the family room with much new news,

"Oz and I just got back from Rome, we were invited to his uncles Villa, I hadn't been to Rome for a while it was great! I am finding out everybody else in his family is rich!"

Staring at Oz with a look like 'what's up with you.'

Oz, squirming a little,

"Come on, we're not rich just comfortable."

Tamra smiling "You know I am just messing with ya. We stayed at his Villa west of Rome that overlooks the Mediterranean, and we drank 'Ouzo' that stuff is fun!"

Listening to her story, Tayas found herself feeling like a real mother all of a sudden, positioning herself to admonish her daughter for overindulging in every way.

Looking at Qwe thinking what now, how are we going to get her alone? The answer soon presented itself, Tamra already refilling her glass and announcing,

"Hay we are going to run out, would my handsome boyfriend run to the store? If you would get two, and one for the hosts."

"Your wish is my wish, my Princess."

A spontaneous utterance of laughter between Tayas & Qwe made Tamra defensibly ask,

"What's so funny?"

Qwe "Well, you have him schooled right…"

Oz asked for any other requests before leaving, with no additions ventured, he left.

Tayas was very nervous, she was going to just lay everything out. So, she grabbed Tamra and Qwe, sat them down and…. staring straight at Tamra, holding her hands,

"I am your mother."

Tamra "Yea I know that, just because you two are married you sort of always treated me like that, it's ok. I don't mind, you think I am going too fast with Oz?"

Tayas "No, listen to me! I am your mother and Qwe is your father!"

Tamra, "Cool…. You guys smoking weed? I'd like some…."

With a tolerant curious smile,

Qwe "No …Tamra, look at me. You know the experiments we have been testing over at our work, we have unintentionally traveled to a different world where we are a family, your sister's names are Lyka and Carisa!"

Tamra "Wow, you guys are on something better than weed, I don't think I want to jump on it this time since Oz is here, but thanks."

Tayas mildly frustrated looking at Qwe,

"How were we going to do this again?"

Qwe shrugged his shoulders, with a smile,

"She is your daughter…"

"Listen! We are not on anything! You remember Chemistry and Physics; you have a degree! We found a way to get there and back! And by the way, you are a real Princess!"

Tamra, calmly gulping her drink now, sitting down…

"Ok… I'll bite, better make it quick thou, I don't want Oz to hear all the strangeness in this new family quite yet."

Tayas, "All this has been just as difficult for us too. This has hit us both really hard, but it's true! Your father and I have been there and back, and all we know we will tell you, there isn't enough time right now.

We wanted to tell you before we made a mistake. For now, if we can be as normal as possible until we can talk, oh, by the way, I am a Fairy."

Tamra couldn't contain herself any longer and burst out laughing!
"Wow! it must be really good stuff! ha-ha!"

At that, Tayas pointed at her glass and floated over it to Tamra. Tamra stopped mid laugh and staring ....unconsciously dropping the glass she was holding, it shattered on the floor and then she plucked the floating glass out of the air, her face was a lit with a frozen "O."

"Did you put something in the wine? Wait a while! I brought it…Wow, that's pretty fuckin cool!"

Tayas pointing at the glass pieces on the floor grouped it all together, picked it up and floated them over to the trash.

Tamra, "Wow! Do I get to do that?"

Qwe "Possibly, you still need to talk with the 'Lady of the Lake.'"
Tamra passionately stated,

"No Way! The 'Lake Lady' like in King Arthur and Merlin and that chick, aah…what's her name…"

With some smiles an small laughs,

"For now, yes way!"

Only on infrequent occasions could Tamra ever be silenced completely. She didn't know what to do. She hugged her mother for the first time, as well as her father. Which upon Oz's return, found Tamra in his embrace with tears of joy.

Oz "It's your birthday! That's what all the extra is for! Happy birthday Qwe!"

Deciding to leave it at that, Tamra rebounded with,
"About time! My glass broke, and it's time for a refill!"

Tayas starting to clean up the rest of the glass by hand, (old fashioned way) Tamra edged in saying,

"I got it Tayas, ops's, mom…?"

Both were kneeling down, looking at each other with new eyes, a-first and now entirely different feeling.

Standing with fresher smiles and hugs, enjoying the evening in an entirely new light.

Of course, Tamra & Tayas got together on the following day and filled the afternoon and evening with a lot of different insight from father, mother and daughter. A slightly different kind of smile and a kindred kind of laughter.

Tayas now wanted to get in touch with Mera to introduce Tamra. Tuesday afternoon in Dr. Mera's office, there were new revelations for all three. After pleasantries,

Mera "This news will reaffirm great confidence in our effort. I was unaware of your mother's presence until she introduced herself by chance. Now, with one of the three here in my presence has certainly stopped the direction we were headed and started to give us a solid positive hope.

I will explain in detail at another time, my wish is to make you two comfortable with what knowledge you have newly acquired. Also, regarding the history, as I talked with the other Dr.'s I forgot to mention that I have transverse or phased with a group of 12.

Possibility on the next trip Qwe, Tayas, Tamra, Rym and myself maybe, I am familiar with the dialect and runes of the time. You had mentioned that Qwe had taken pictures of a book in the cave, if I could, I would like to take a look at them, it would help."

Tamra "Excuse me, I don't mean to sound corny or right out of the movies, but we are the good guys, right?"

Mera smiling "You wouldn't have been able to even ask that question if we weren't. The good thought as you put it, never would have entered your mind, yes we are the 'good' guys."

Together, their ideas and plans started to coheir. Dr. Mera was also on the Board at the London Archaeological Museum and had a trove of artifacts of the period.

Back in her office, our girl Tamra was losing her mind! She couldn't keep herself on track, or so she thought, she felt she was on the verge of calling Oz and telling him everything! It was tenuous for her, but she was making it for now.

Chapter Fourteen

As their phase time approached, everything was coming together and finding order in its place. Standing around the test cage with the crystal in place, it started. All the others present knew the feeling, Tamra was staring at her mother, Tayas took her hand. The pleasant humming/vibrating washed over, then everything blurred, phasing out…then landed, phasing … in.

Of course, Tamra was first up,
"Wow! I gotta do that again! Wow!"
Mera, being concerned about the time, asked Rym to accompany her to the cave, finding their flashlights, they headed in. Tayas on the other hand, was watching Tamra trying to take in as much as possible, unable to stay in one place. Standing back amused, she couldn't help laughing to herself.
Tamra's soliloquy was excitable,
"Wow, CK-out that lake it is blue! Look at this place, Wow! All the trees, where are we… oh, yeah, Scotland somewhere, who cares, I am going swimming don't even think about stopping me. I gotta see if you're jiving me…ok, you men people stay here, I'm on a mission!"
And kept on talking as they both walked to the lake. Tamra was out of her clothes and about to jump in, Tayas was half undressed when she stopped Tamra.
"Hold it, I have to be first."
Tamra looked very impatient waiting with her hands on her hips, tapping her fingers…
"Any time…. Mom…"
"Well, I guess, one, two three jump!"
At first very cold then…
"Welcome Tayas, you have found a daughter!"
" Yes! Ma 'Lady, I wanted to introduce her if that is agreeable, she is very excited to have this chance!"
"She is welcome."

Tayas putting her head just above the water,

"She'd like to meet you…"

''Wow!'' splash…

Tayas took her hand and tried to calm her, no good. She shot back up, then under,

"Ma 'Lady this is my daughter Tamra."

"Welcome Tamra"

That sent Tamra back to the surface of the water and,

"Did you hear that! where are you, oh yea."

Back under Tayas was thinking,

"She is full of energy."

Nyneve "Tamra, slow your thoughts, you will see soon, and be able to breathe with me."

"I'll be right back…"

Up… breath…. down

"Sorry. I'm back."

"I will help calm you both, listen to my voice Tamra, think on that. I gather some knowledge but not all. We are trying to locate your sisters. There are so many different worlds I cannot go to all. This is where Alda and Merlin must aid us, I know Mera, she will be of great help."

Tamra couldn't stand it…" a, aum excuse me miss 'Lake Lady' do I get to pick up stuff with my fingers?"

Tayas was embarrassed if you can be underwater…

"Tamra, that's not a question you should ask."

Nyneve "Tamra, it will be so. Your gift is of a medium order, but like your mother, it will improve."

"Oh Wow, cool thanks!"

Tayas "I must apologize for…"

Nyneve " Have no concerns, she seems a delight. Qwe and Mera are waiting, go with caution."

Tamra "I can see you now… dang your pretty!"

Tayas "Ha Tamra!... Thank you, MA' Lady."

Upon surfacing Tamra,

"Wowaow, hay dad, turn around I gotta get dressed!"

Turning around he smiled at Mera
"Kids!"
Both talking among themselves as they dressed
"Hey mom, ck. this out!"
She pointed her finger at her backpack that was by Qwe,
levitating it to herself.
" I.... Wow!"

Standing on the shore of the blue lake, staring at her fingers
she had a look of complete command!
Qwe with a loving smile
"There will be no peace in our house!"
Small laughs.

Chapter Fifteen

Their collective overnight camping idea was to spend it in the cave, then on to Sterling at daylight. Qwe set himself to making things as comfortable as possible.

Mera "I can't tell exactly what time we've landed in until we leave the glen that will be evident as we move out on the road. For the moment, I would like to look into the rune book."

She grabbed a light, and into the next cave. Qwe and Rym set off for firewood which was in plenty. Returning with arms loaded, Rym assessing the size and height of the caves, decided the second room in the system would be allot easier to warm.

Tamra was next to impossible at dinner, playing with the fire, playing with her dads food, warming a pot of water over the fire for tea, 'look, no hands mom!'

It was a wonderful light feeling she unknowingly spun that first evening that set everyone in pleasant sprites for it.

The Company slept as comfortably as a heavy blanket, the ground and dried grass would permit through the night.

Morning met them with some clouds, not too threatening and hiking out of Alva glen and heading south to Sterling.

Rym was deferring to Mera when asked questions; one was yes, they could speak English but quietly. Taking Tayas & Tamra aside, she told them in all seriousness, in fact, that if they were caught using their gifts, they would be branded as Witches. In some circles at the time, would be a very unhealthy idea.

Mera hoped she remembered where the farm was to stay the next night, it would take two days to the Castle.

Off they started, Tayas & Tamra were enjoying the hike down the glen with little waterfalls and curious little twists in the trail.

Everywhere there seemed a soft naturally whispering, along the creek the trees dripping with morning dew, birds with quiet inquisitive looks. Mera had to remind them to speak Latin if they met someone, not English (For the reader: again, Latin, Gaelic. French was questionable most of the time. Those were the three excepted languages during this period. It did matter what location you were in, or who you spoke what language to. Gaelic and Latin was common.)

Qwe, Rym, Mera were soft-spoken not much talk, on the other hand, Tamra couldn't stop with questions, Tayas had to remind her that she hadn't been out of the glen this far, so it was all new territory to her.

Their goal today was about 15 km the route is reasonably flat, so, it shouldn't be too bad.

All were glad to see the farm come into view, Mera hoped the farmer would remember her, she greeted him and ask for space for the night, (she spoke Scotts Gaelic), and the company was awarded the barn. He vaguely remembered her, telling them about no fires in the barn, were his only rules.

With new oats in the stalls, their night was softer than the cave. A small fire outside the door was just right to warm some tea, so far, no rain yet, but the farmer said that might change tomorrow.

Yes, guess what…Tamra was up first and asking,

"Hey, ya know, I have a question."

Tayas, packing things on her knees in the hay, looking at her daughter smiling,

"Why am I not surprised!"

Tamra "Why are we going to the Castle, what's the big deal there?"

"Mera has more people she knows and apparently will help us."

Tamra "Help us to do what?"

Tayas briefly pausing and thinking,

"That is an excellent question, let's ask,

Mera…. are we to meet someone or …"?

Mera "Yes, I am sorry to keep this vague, please trust me, this has to do with all gifts. That is as much as I should say at the moment... ears…"

In saying that, she pointed around possible listing places in the barn. Tayas & Tamra understood.

Mera mentioned the farmer had given them some biscuits, and a letter to be delivered to the kitchen in the Castle.

Covering more kilometers than the day before, they quickly were in the market in the early afternoon, and down a familiar hall to Rym. Mera asked them all to go down the same alternate hall that Dr. J & Rym had been in and told to wait there. Mera, passing on into the depths of the kitchen, people in the midst of preparation for the evening. She went right up to one of the peasants, slapped her on her back,

"Well, aww is ohme?"

Alda slowly turning "Ah, Mera aven't seen the likes of ye for a month of fortnights!"

Mera, " Just so, good ta see ya, we should have a geten together soon, tonight good?"

Alda "Fine!"

Mera "I've four that av' traveling with me, ok? Still in the same aush?"

Alda "Just so, aven't moved a spud!"

Mera "Fine!"

Mera, arriving back in the hall that the others were waiting in, found them a little ill at ease. Saying that a man had passed, and had a touch floating in front as he passed,

Mera very casually,

"That might be Ambrose's, his rooms are in that direction when he is here."

Tamra "Wait, what…. That was the real Merlin?"

"I'm not entirely sure, but we will find out soon enough."

Leading off to the market in the square, Mera wasn't sure, but she thought she was recognized by a person she didn't want to talk to just yet. Not wanting to cause attention, good or bad, they passed through the main gates.

It of course, was starting to rain, so they hurried down the long sloping hill and into the busy village. Into some muddy partially cobbled streets, with chilly sparking raindrops from all the roof eves overhead, landing with a punctuated splat! And on through a number of back dingy allies.

Pausing to knock at the front door of a distressed, nondescript small row home, was slowly greeted by a man. The two recognized each other instantly, not talking, inviting all inside, introductions were made after the door was latched.

Ushered into sitting at a large rough rectangle table, were served tea by a little boy. Mera's first statement had everyone in her group wondering,

"I've welcome tidings, Tayas & her daughter Tamra have met the 'Lady of the lake' and were restored their gifts, I would wait for Alda if ye mind Rune."

Rune "No use in telling stories twice! Would anyone of ya like a biscuit? Goats milk?"

Tayas, "Yes a biscuit please, thank you for your hospitality."

"Think nothing of it MA' Lady, Alda will be here shortly, Rym, Tayas, Tamra & Qwe were waiting for Mera to fill them in with regards to speaking so freely,

"We are like kind, meaning they are gifted and are very involved with the fight to keep magic only on this world. The men fight in terrible wars, I should tell all of you there is a person who is… no, I must tell you all the history, but that must wait. We will stay here for two nights, then Rym wants to be back at the cave one day early."

Rym, "We must consider each phase event unique, and be very careful, thank you, Mera. Tamra, I know you, and your mom have one hundred questions, and they will be answered. All this is why we wanted you to come with us, we felt it would be easier to consider the answers after you've met all the people involved."

Tamra, was distantly in the conversation, she was absently looking at Rym, seemingly for the first time,

"You know what? You are my grandfather!"

Rym, Qwe & Tayas especially laughed with delight,

Tayas "Ha, did you understand what your grandfather just said?"

"Yes, Mother deer Wow, that is still so very strange now, hay, do you remember having us three?"

Tayas "No, and I don't like it, I miss holding babies, dressing them every which way, combing all of your beautiful blond hair…"

Qwe breaking into the conversation "Feeding and changing diapers all day and night, never sleeping…"

Tayas "Well, hmm, would you mind if I comb your hair once in a while?"

Tamra "Don't be stupid, we've been doing that all of our adult lives anyway!"

"Guess so huh, ok you are right, I'll think of something else I missed, Mera, do you have any idea how all that transpired, the whole interchange how…."

"Yes, I am very aware of your family history, but not yet, (door opening) this might be Alda."

And so it was, she had brought a friend that Mera knew, so introductions all around again. The boy was Alda's Son and helped to ready themselves for the evening. Ladies in one room, men in the front room, starting a fire, letting time float, Rune smoking his pipe offered crude cigars to Qwe & Rym.

Qwe " I am very much in your debt, having all of us here, we will try to blend into the background out of your way, disappear."

Rune "That's one of ye gifts?"

Qwe smiling "No, actually my wife and daughter are gifted."

Rune "Ha! dat 'Lady of the Lake' she is always passin' gifts off ta women, I tell you, next time you are by a lake don't tell Tayas, just jump straight in and look at what ye' get! ha!"

Rym "Now, I think you have something there!"

Rune "Yea…. I shouldn't tug at her hair, I truly have nuten but high regard fr the lady, not all men or woman get a gift, it is set down by God! ...sorry, that will make for more questions for ya. I understand yu are newly 'ere, and you plan to go off to other worlds ta find more 'o family."

At that, Qwe looked at Rym very questionable,

Rune "Oh well then, I've o'r stepped myself, let me tell yu most of yu'r questions will be answered at our evening sit. Let me say this, I ave not gone ta other places, but Mera and Alda ave, I will tell yu true, Qwe, Tayas an especially Tamra have changed the game board so to speak."

Coming into the gathering room, Alda in her way, had a feeling that Rune had volunteered too much information,

"At talking out oer much bout things my dear man?"

Rune, "You know o'w I get nervous around folks."

Alda "Yes ma dar'lin I have heard it before, you do better with ya sword & pix in your hand than with ye hair combed an shaken' hands."

Qwe," I did notice a 'saber' above the mantle, epée's' and saber are my choices, very engaging sport."

"Er'e lad, it's a way of life, we con go a round or two, after a bit."

Both were up for it.

Alda, "No there'll be no time for that! We have a good lot to talk about. Come to table all of ya..."

Qwe," Tomorrow maybe?"

Rune "Quite right lad!"

Men laughing, Alda with a scolding look...

"Rune....... Grace if you please!"

Chapter Sixteen

This is a chapter only for justification purposes. Maybe I should ask someone about how to explain all this next bit of history ...."Hey Siri!"

Past history went like this; with the introduction of other earths travelers/phasers or 'Owners' they call themselves, rarely did they come with any good intent. It wasn't known what earth they originated from first, or how many different earths they had been too.

We now would refer to them in a unkind way, pinches, thieves, shit heads, etc.... They acquired what was 'ordered' from whatever world they had landed, certain people and or vast sums of anything that was worth value on these worlds, then take it back to their own.

In this illustration of Tayas & Qwe's daughters that were kidnaped, each one passed into a different earth and historical time. Tamra, just by chance came to this earth T-1 (for the reader: I will enumerate different earths,

T-1, T-3 T-7, etc.

I'll start with T-1 (knowing there is an infinite configuration of earths, gotta start somewhere) So, the first daughter by a mistake of Fidalac 's henchman, Tamra, fell into her mother's lap without either knowing of the other. That mistake in-fact has given the Quest copious amounts of self-assurance and added momentum.

The two girls that remain, somewhere, with the little evidence that was had, didn't give them the exact location of each yet. (For the reader: you think that is weird, are you ready?)

Tayas was 19 years old when the three girls were born. At three years of age a owner/traveler, kidnaped the girls, for large sums of gold, he was instructed to leave behind no trace.

Then coming back and kidnaping Tayas and Qwe, taking them back 13 years, that of course changing their age to that of when she and Qwe were 6 years old, and then advancing forward into T-1 (they were on T-4 at the time)

' Fidalac ' on pain of death demand that all traces be erased.

Now, Tayas and the three were already endowed at birth with their ability to except their gifts when given. Fidalac being unaware of the gifts, was only of one mind; all that was required was their same bloodline must be Royal. He intended to bring Tayas's father Rym, ruin and disorder to his kingdom. So, the three princesses were dispersed on the wind, throughout many random galaxies.

Chapter Seventeen

What Mera then went on to narrate was in the hopeful future for all, Alda started off,

"We, and when I say we, it will include all present. The reinstating of the daughters will start to establish the correct pasterns of each world that have been visited by this 'Fidalac' who has changed that World without a care to any affected.

Tayas, we can be confident, will be able to recognize her daughters, and of course sister Tamra also. Mera told me of how she saw you Tayas, it will be much the same when you meet your girls."

Tayas "Well, why did I not 'see' Tamra, we were at the University and Grad school together, was it because I had no 'sight' then?"

Alda "You had to be reminded by the 'Lady' remember? she told you something of that nature."

Tayas "Yes I do remember, but when Qwe & I went back the first time, I didn't 'see' Tamra that first night, or feel as I do now?"

Mera "It's because you're reawakening was but new, just warming up if you will, and you, both of you will acquire more as you age."

Tamra "Wow, like I can maybe turn my boyfriend into a rich boyfriend?" all laughing,

Mera, "Well, sort of…but that is different, you may ask Ambrosias those questions."

Tayas "Was that him we saw in the storeroom?"

Alda "Yes, he's here for a short time, and t'is because you are here, he will meet with you all tomorrow at the castle. As I was heading home today, he told me he could feel Tayas & Tamra's aura and is needing to talk with Tayas."

That put Tayas in a milled shock,

"The real Merlin… he wants to talk to me?"

Stated unbelievingly.

Alda, "Yes, and let me warn all of you, he is a curious one. His mind may drift, so don't be alarmed if he doesn't address your questions right off, he will get around to them soon enough."

Tamra, "Wow! Can I go too?"

"Aye, he expressly asked for you also."

"No way! really? Wow, I can't wait… should we dress up or something!"

Alda "Ha- ha no, he expects not of the sort, besides what ave you else to ware?"

Tayas "Remember your manners Tamra…unbelievable, now I am sounding like a mother!"

And so, the evening went…

The following crisp morning, Alda, along the way to the castle did a little shopping, off into the woods to collect some herbs fairly common, but useful for a wizard. It gave the group some moments to enjoy the mist that was hovering low in the forest and reflect on the techniques of "Going to the market" in the 12th Century.

Entering the noisy market square, meeting some lingering smells that were easy on the nose, but most weren't. Passing into familiar halls for Rym, walking past the storeroom he and Dr. J had hidden in, and past a few more doors. Alda lightly knocking, then entering a room that had the appearance of living chaos abounding!

Scrolls, books, pots and jars, everywhere in large & small piles! It had the look you might expect of age-old accumulation of dust on dust.

Sitting at a table bussing himself writing, was a gray haired mid-sized man. Alda walked over and taped lightly on the shoulder of the only resident of the room.

"Not, not now… oh Alda, yes, they have come, yes…"

Turning he stood, Alda was starting introductions when, in an evenly timed voice filled with significant understanding...

"Qwe & Tayas welcome your majesties, you Tayas are the easiest of all, no one forgets your smile my Queen. (He faced)

Princes Tamra: you I can see, have translated your mother and father's fine lines into a unique beauty of no compare! Well, that is, we haven't found your sisters yet, so I will make my final decision at that moment."

Tamra, aw struck "Thank you very kind and knowledgeable sir, Wow!"

Merlin appearing strangely uncertain,

"Wow, what is this?"

Tayas "Forgive her sir, a funny phase from our earth, it's a bit of a habit."

Merlin was thoughtfully pondering, "Well, then, Wow…."
Smiles all around.

Alda "I have a little branny for your tea, stopped by the woods."

Merlin "Thank you Alda, well now, let me have a look If I may Tayas, I would like your hands"

Tayas stepping up to the table,

"I must say, the last time I saw you, your attire was a bit nobler, but this is a good costume, yes…and your eyes….

so, the 'Lady' tells me Tamra has also been nicely met, as well as yourself.

(Dismissing Tayas) Tamra, the same if you please"
Exchanging places and passing, Tayas whispered,

"Be good!"

"Of course,"

With a quick frown at her mother, taking her place in front of Merlyn.

"Yes, you are the first born, but you alone hold a very heavy role because you were found first. Your light heart will counter the low places…… hold that thought, I must get a gift!"

Turning to a shelf of dusty wooden boxes of every size, returned with a small very beautiful Walnut box lightly tarnished with age. It held three bands of gold around the top edge, placing it in Tamra's hands,

"This was a birth gift from your father and mother." Tamra was very perplexed, looking at him,
"Can I open it?"

Merlin "Well… that's what presents seem to be for…"
With a smile and a wave of his hand, turning to sit, she opened the chest lined with silk, was a silver crown.

Tamra "Oh my god, that's a real crown!"

"The Carpenter for your wooden box was your father, and the crown was made in Edinburgh by the Royal Craftsman. Qwe, please do the honors…"

Not being really sure what was intended,

Qwe "Yes?"
Merlin, looking confused himself,

"Well…. Crown your daughter, Princess Tamra!"
Qwe, quickly thinking kingly,

"Of course, yes, crown my daughter, Wow! … Now I am saying it!"

"Don't be nervous daddy!"
Striking up a kingly pose;

"I Qwe Rtyuiop, Father of Tamra, crown her 'Princess Tamra."

As he was saying thus, he placed the crown on her now Royal crest. Tamra quickly asked Tayas if she brought a hand mirror, laughs, Tayas coming close, tears, (hugs, lv it).

Tamra "I can't wait to get a selfie of this the way I am dressed."

Merlin "You will be able to 'travel' with it until all is restored. I must give you a heady warning, it cannot be lost! After we have set everything wright, it will only be available in this world.

Well…. we must get on to less enjoyable things."
Merlin turning towards another shelf,

"Let me show you something of another world. This is what you think it is, a crystal similar to the one from my cave that brought you here. This one is entirely different. I have an idea of what earth and where, but I can't be certain.

My attempts at traveling to this other world have failed, here I can use my magic but that must coincide with a heavy thunderstorm, that happens on occasion here. On your earth it seems to happen much easier, you must tell me how that is sometime.

For now, I must ask one of you to explore, not Tayas or Tamra, they must be safe until we have located Lyka, Carisa, at that time it will be of most importance that Tayas & Tamra then travel to confirm the identity of her sisters."

Tamra, "Excuse me mister sir, umm... I have to go into two new worlds and just find them?

Most people in the city don't even know who lives next door, don't mean to be rude, how am I going ta do that?''

Merlyn "Don't worry about that now, it my responsibility to find the world's first.

I'll have Mera introduce you to others that are close to the times they are in and will be of suitable help. At the moment I would like to find out how you travel!"

Rym was more than happy to explain to Merlin how the Hadron Collider works, so together they moved to the next room, Mera asked to join them. Alda was off to the kitchen, getting some water and tea, of course, biscuits for all.

After a small sit with a biscuit in hand, Tamra needed to be reminded she still had her crown on and would draw a lot of unwanted attention when they step out.

Tamra, "Oh, thanks, I guess it suites me, I was getting to use to it."

Tayas "Oh-sister give us a break! Here, I have a large bag, you can put dad's case in with your new adornment."

Tamra "Wow, dad's, mom's, gramps, wizards, picking stuff up with my finger, who wants to leave?"

Tayas, "What about Oz?"
That slowed her down,

"Oh yea, what do you think, or not. I'm not going to tell him, he probably will take me flying one day, and do a role, then to be nice I'll have to say, wow keno. Then, back on the ground I could pick him up and role him with one finger."

Tayas, "I am going to remind you to get a grip on yourself, this is very serious. Finding your sisters is going to put a lot on you."

Alda, "Not just them, but the people on four different worlds!"
Tamra excepting it, sat down, feeling a bit introspective.

Alda, "Ti's a very big order but as Ambrosias sz; yur light heart wl see yu through, duny dwell much onit nuw."

Rym, Merlin and Mera were explaining how the Collider functioned as best they could in more of a broad sense, not needing to get into fine detail. Still, he was astonished at the power alone that could be generated, then focused, and meet together at such speed!

As he in-turn, had a hard time trying to explain the verbal math inherent in all his magic.

All parties were equally impressed and confused at the same time. Mera, Rym & Qwe were told how Merlin had 'traveled' staying on this earth (T-2) to Arthur's time. That would be the future of Merlyn's and explaining that he is a physique-shifter, so he could easily assume the look of younger or older.

Wanting to get back to his studies, he bid farewell for now to all. Alda, had requested him at dinner, since their Company was leaving on the morrow, all was set.

A rainy afternoon loitered into the evening, a light knock was at the door, Alda answering found an old lady standing there.
With not a word she was let in.

Alda "A bit damp tonight ea, warm yourself at the fire."
The living area was populated with the traveling company, Qwe offered his seat by the warm fire.

"Thank you Qwe."
Qwe," Have we met before?"

"Yes, this morn" he/she said with short words
"Merlin?"

"My service is yours..."
Tayas & Tamra in shock again,

Tamra "Wow, are u... can u, how can you do that!"

Merlin "I tell you lassie, it's a potion, and is a smidgen uncomfortable to change so I stay as you see me. I'm meeting with some traveling Royals back at the castle and must assume a different appearance."

They were just staring at him, arms resting on the splintered table, still Tamra had a question...

"Can I do that?"

"In a word... No."

Tamra "oh."

Merlin, "Be patient my princes, next on your gifts will probably be fire, as it is a matter that will come along for the two of you, let me show you."

He looked at a lit candle on the table, pointed with two fingers, then slightly brushed his hand side to side, the candle went out. Then pointing with two fingers again, then pealing out the rest of his fingers, puff it was lit.

Merlin "Tamra, give it a try."

She looked nervous but pointing at the candle with two fingers then a small swipe, knocked it over, then spread her fingers and the whole table was on fire! Merlin easily waved his (or her) hand and it was out!

"Maybe we should wait on perfecting your gift, you also, Tayas."

Tamra "Sorry everyone, hum... beginners mistake"

As dinner moved on, the company started talking about the next trip, getting details written down (Rym brought a small note and felt pen, that had everybody looking at) all seemed to be set.

Merlin bid good travels to each, paying special attention to Tamra, Merlin (Merlyn sp. fem?)

"Have a good step back, be warned about the gifts, they will be a help, use them sparingly. Oh yes, practice fire outside, and away from other eyes, Tayas, those words would also benefit you also."

Chapter Eighteen

The morning sent them out the door with broken rain clouds that left the puddles on the road brimming over with murky water. It had rained most of the night and persisted lightly into the afternoon. Each one under rain tarps and in a world of their own, reflecting on each drop of rain that managed to slip by on a shoulder or neck and remind them how cold and wet they were. It was with little talk along the road until the welcome farmhouse came into view, the door was knocked on once again.

The company was offered a meager dinner inside the warm house for the farming family to hear any new or different stories of Merlin. Mera didn't want all to be told, thinking only stories of the Castle. This night was offered to them inside the home, the barn roof was leaking far too much for comfort.

Next morning, tea & oat cakes and out the door, the Sun had made a good appearance easing the hiking day on to Alva glen. Tamra was at Tayas's side discussing anything that could be thought of.

The men and Mera were in talks of kingdoms changing hands, who's who and the like. The road was a very wide path, so three could walk abreast and talk story with ease.

Chapter Nineteen

Arriving back at the base of Alva glen, Rym and Mera now in the lead, noticed a man riding away on a horse heading in the direction of Campbell Castle. The company hid and stayed hidden until the rider was out of sight.

Mera, "I wonder of that."

Rym, "What concerns you?"

Mera, "et's go on ta' camp ta see."

Rym wanted to note:

"You are getting the accent quickly; it does seem to be comfortable to the ear."

Mera "Ta Rym..."

Rym "Are you worried about something amiss?"

Mera "Maybe, et's go on up an see."

Approaching the cave, Qwe had his light and checked on their provisions and found nothing amiss. Mera still had an uneasy feeling. Each of the company went about their business getting settled for the night.

Rym & Qwe decided to head out under the pretense of collecting firewood, it was the finish of a good day, still warm Rym had a plan of his own to follow Rune's advice. Qwe had the same idea.

Heading over to the lake taking his stuff off, Qwe wasn't going to be out done and did likewise, both men grinning at each other.

They both jumped in, each were anticipating the same anointment, there was no sound, both surfaced

Rym "It's freezing! one more try, let me go first"

Rym dunked under again and was met with the identical manifestation as Tayas had seen.

Nyneve "Welcome your highness, I didn't want to speak to others out of turn, I wanted to address your Majesty first. Qwe may come."

Rym surfaced and included Qwe, "Come on then."

"Welcome your highness, are you both comfortable?"
Qwe & Rym "One more breath, up and back"

Nyneve, "I am sure that Tayas has told you to just relax and listen to my voice. We in this world of magic, are under attack and it is your two kingdoms that have suffered the most in this matter. It will be put on your shoulders to right the wrong, your entire family must be found."

Rym "I thank you for this opportunity to straighten out this disorder. I will do the utmost I can, and I know Qwe will also 'Ma'- lady'"

Qwe, "Finding my two daughters is now foremost. Any and all help will be greatly appreciated, I thank you very much 'Lady of the lake."

"Ambrosius has given you some good direction, it's up to you to carry on for a while, we will meet again, I am being called." Getting out of the water Qwe mentioned,

"It wasn't cold when she talked."

Rym "I found it pleasant as well, now I must see if I can outdo my granddaughter."

Pointing at his clothes, Qwe did as much, and two pairs of paints floated towards the laughing men, Qwe had an idea while dressing,

"Let's not tell the girls yet, we can say we just splashed our faces"

Rym "A fine thought, this will give us quiet an edge!"

Heading towards the trees for firewood, passing Tayas and Tamra on their way from the cave, Tamra asked Qwe,

"Did you guys fall in?"
Qwe "Just splashing our faces, we will get the fire lit."

"No no, let me practice! Really, ok?!"

Tamra said they were just getting water; they would be right there.

"Alright, we'll wait then"

Tayas was at the water's edge with her hands in, was wondering about the 'Lady' Tamra knelt and did likewise

"Welcome my Queen and Princess you have Merlin's council, remember when traveling do not expose your gifts openly. I wish you good travels"

The two thanked the 'Lady' filling the clay pots, headed back to their cave for the night. The men patiently waiting around an unlit fire, Tamra came jogging in, she couldn't wait. Everybody was in the middle cave standing before the pile of sticks, Tamra was looking very serious, she pointed with two fingers then opening her hand with a swish type of movement, the sticks flew everywhere!

"Wow! Sorry I'll get-um, one more mom, ok?"
Mildly blushing, collecting wood from a wide circle

Tayas "How about start with a small pile?"

Tamra "Sure ya, ok here we go."

This time, she didn't do a girly swish, but did peel open her hand just right and it worked! A small fire neatly formed, quite happy with herself she sat down with the look of a conquering hero,

"Ha! Nothing to it! I just needed less girly swish!"

Tayas felt she couldn't be out done by her own kids, concentrating with two fingers, subtlety small move then closed all her fingers. It worked! The fire went out, next she reversed the charm and poof a perfect fire!

Tamra "Show off! you cheated, you practiced somewhere."

Tayas "Remember, I have had mine longer dear daughter, so maybe that's it! Ha-ha."

Mera had been searching with Rym in the other rooms of the cave to find the book which was still in-place, moving into the deeper part, they came upon one of the cave walls incrusted with crystals like the one in the lab. Merlin had told them about that room and mentioning that they should quench whatever light source, for quite a spectacle.

It really was amazing! Different reflections everywhere!

They looked at each other to say,

"Wow!"

And both laughed.

Everybody met back around the fire Rym was first to note,

"What happened here it's a mess!"

Tamra "Oh, gramps, my fault! I was starting the fire and it all went everywhere! Of course, you should have seen mom, miss perfect."

Just for effect she stuck her tong out at Tayas. chuckle, chuckle. (For the reader: yes, Tamra has a PhD in Mathematics)

They have had a long day, their savory beef jerky, biscuit's & tea tasted extra especially good. Time to literally 'Hit the hay.'

Good night to all, Rym suggested they all go to the very back of the cave tomorrow before we leave, but didn't tell them why, just for amusement.

Today, this afternoon 1:00 would be the departure time (maybe) so, after Tamra started the breakfast fire, with not as much mess, tea & biscuits and jerky were had, then the tour.

All were impressed as they should be, small colorful crystal prisms all above them on the cave ceiling,

Close to their travel time all gathered close together at the cave entrance, Tayas & Tamra hand in hand...and it did start.

At the start, Rym looking back at the forest close by the glen, noticed a man that maybe looked or dressed the same as the person they all saw a day ago. He was watching them phase, then was running at them as soon as they started. He was able to come into the circle, Rym tried to push him away, but to no avail, things were starting to re-focus the lab.

Rym was first "Who are you! What the diva are you doing!"

The rest of the company has just taken notice, Qwe came up quickly grabbing another arm!

"Wait good sirs!"

He was speaking a loose Latin and had the others at a loss for a minute, all were familiar with the langue but hadn't used that form of it for a few years. Trying to recall a word or two to answer with,

Dr. Rym set his mind and sorted out what he could. He was older, dressed in the time period, sitting him down, the rest gathered around as Rym did his best.

"What is your name?"
"Anthony" Acting a little afraid,

Rym "Where are you from?"

"Rome."

Rym had to really consider how to piece together the next phrase in the appropriate tongue

"What time in history?"

Anthony, looking confused, Rym tried again with a deferent phrase,

Anthony "I am with Pius Pilot"

Everybody looked at each other, trying to think of the correct Historical timelines to put a recognizable face and date on it.

Qwe "Hold it, let me get the translator"

Returning, the first thing Anthony asked for was food and water. The travelers had plenty left over that made that easy. Rym & Mera being suspicious, took Tayas aside to tell her not to give him water from the lake, save that for analyses.

Now, Dr. J started in deep conversation with Anthony and Rym was asking more about how he got from Rome to where he was in the first place.

Looking as if he was in a panic, saying that he collected rocks and crystals, and had found some new crystals.
Hurrying back to his room (in Rome) during a terrible storm, he sat down and was comparing the two.

The one he already had, holding that with his new one, decided to wash the new and the old in a river that was close by.

"Crouching down at the river, I was almost hit by lightning! Next thing, I was where you found me, outside of the cave. Walking to a castle, I traded some small crystals for a horse and food. Two days later I found you.

I put the old crystal in my pocket and was holding the new one in my hand when I woke up by the cave. I have thought I have lost senses and my mind was no more."

Mera was holding back something but would not say anything as yet. As things started to wind down, Rym and Mera were talking by themselves,

"It's my opinion we must be very careful, we need to lock our crystal away somewhere. He speaks too well he could be a 'owner' I don't like it, he's too comfortable with the phasing."

Rym "Yes, we have a safe, and that's part of our measures, and yes, it goes back in right now."

Taking the crystal out of the test rack and into the storage room locking it away, Mera meet Rym on his return and told him that the man was watching his every move the whole time.

Rym, thinking he needed to tell the others, to use the translator to invite the stranger to use the bathroom and clean up if he liked. Showing him robes on the hook, and there is a small room here he is welcome to relax in. When the water was running, Rym got everybody together. Mera updated everybody, Dr. J was planning on staying overnight anyway, working late, so he would watch him.

They all didn't want him outside to explore or make good an escape.

The issue now, what were they going to do with him? He did have a crystal from Rome, they possibly could easily send him off. Rym's thought was with the availability of a different crystal, with unlimited earths and this fellow here now, this might be a connection to, and a possibility of getting closer to one of the daughters.

Knowing the 'phasing-affect' could not be known to all peoples of other worlds, this has the potential of establishing a "neighborhood" or adding variables of visitations from the same group.

Without much farther assessment, he decided to personally take 'Anthony' back to Rome under the guise of locating a princess.

Knowing Merlin gave them another crystal to 'explore with,' decided that would have to wait, his presents here was too much of a risk on so many fronts.

Dr. J was made available of the information and agreed they must do something with the questionable person that invited himself in on the phasing group.

Chapter Twenty

The afternoon was moving on into night, everyone had changed and was headed out to their different homes. Tamra was going to spend the night at Tayas's. Rym asked if he could come over and bring dinner. (Italian)

After first stopping at the restaurant, thinking on the issues of the next trip, and how he was going to map an outline of travel for the group.

Rym arrived with his arms loaded, ushering himself in to Qwe's & Tayas's home while setting things down, he happily noticed Tamra with her crown on,

"I see you are looking oh so much the princess, it suits you well."

Tamra smiling "Thanks gramps, or is it your highness?"

"Just Rym or gramps thanks. I hope everybody is in good health, I have lasagna and a salad for our dining pleasure."

All settled in with oil and Italian bread and lasagna, wine in hand, Rym launched into his plan,

"It is my intention to take Anthony back to Rome as soon as possible, we must be rid of him. Mera thinks he could possibly be working for an 'Owner,' so I'll take him back. Qwe, it would be of great help if you would assist me."

Tayas, "I am going too, I haven't been to Rome for a long time."

Rym "This isn't a light outing, and I don't need a lot of company…"

"Dad, remember what Merlin said, that Tamra & I will know my daughter by sight, so we have to start somewhere."

"You, I know, won't give up, but Tamra will stay here, I too will reflect on what Merlin said, Tamra is to be protected."

Tamra "That's a bummer, I could have shone you all the sights!"

Tayas "In a horse drawn market cart? This will be what century, I don't know, and I do know a little history, and I have been there ten or so times. I think we'll be ok; you stay put here."

Tamra "Yes mother dear…"

The Hadron Collider was going to run 4 tests, that were going to run one hour apart then 4 days later, 4 more at the same rate. This was to start in two days, their new addition Anthony seemed pleased, he was asked about the weather, cloths and money in Rome at the time he left. Also, Rym explained that his crystal was going to be left behind, his answer was,

"I have more.''

For Rym and Mera, it was a understated admission of previous transits. Everyone for their part was kind to him, but not engaging for long periods of time.

Mera, had requested to be included and Rym was quietly delighted. So, the company of this trip included Rym, Mera, Tayas, Qwe and Anthony.

So much for Rym's desire to keep it simple. All things were concluded, everything was very much the same as past transfers. Anthony made his interest known, still wanting to go outside "To see more" his requests were not given into.

Tayas, talking quietly with her dad kinda got a feeling, lightly smiling,

"Hay dad, kinda happy Mera is coming along?"

Rym "To get in front of where you are heading, yes, we have seemed to become, how shall we say, 'comfortable' with each other. She is a few years younger, in the same situation as I am."

Tayas "I think it's great Dad, it's not healthy to be alone."

With that pleasant understanding between them, they said good night.

(Hugs, daughters…lv it.)

Chapter Twenty-one

Phase day, all travelers in place, Dr. J handing Rym a print-out of the test times & dates. He mentioned it might be best to wait and not come back the next hour, but in one of the following times, he had included dates for next week, just in case.

All five present, the vibrating harmonic resonating started …. they were here… then gone! Phasing back into Rome materializing on the bank of a small stream.

Anthony, without a word quickly turned and ran, heading over a bridge mingling through the crowded streets, quickly separating himself from the others.

Everybody seemed pleasantly surprised and satisfied to be free of the encumbrance.

Mera "And good riddance to you!"

It was late afternoon getting dark, Qwe was trying to position themselves on an old Map. They all were familiar with Rome in their Time, but not here in the 12Th century. Qwe, thinking he had found themselves by the River Tiber,

"That obviously large round building way over there looks like The Colosseum"

It was visible looking over the tops of nearby buildings, he figured a Kilometer or two.

All things felt semi familiar, and they started to discuss the departure time, staying longer than 1 hour, possibility till first of the week. It was thought they should at least try to find one of the girls, not knowing really how to proceed.

They would look for an Inn or something…

They all headed off in the direction of the Coliseum, Rym still looking at the map.

Rym "I will hazard an easy guess at the Language of the day being Latin. That should present some interest to the people we address."

Qwe "I have the translator and ear plugs, I can wrap part of my shirt around my head to disguise it, or we can try our French first."

Rym "Let's stick with Latin, French might be understood, but we want to blend in."

Latin was a very unnatural for Rym and Qwe.

The band of newcomers wandered along a street close to the river and found it not very likable. Moving over a bridge up away from the water's edge, they came upon a piazza with a sculptured fountain, people milling about with an overall pleasant congenial appearance.

The group sat down around the fountain, Rym and Qwe set off to find an Inn. Cruising around Piazza Navona, they happen on a place that looked more like a bar, Rym stepped in and tried his best Latin on a man behind a large table that doubled for a front desk,

"Would have you two rooms?"

The interchange sort of went over ok, after a time the two came to an understanding.

Two silver pieces seemed to include dinners and some potables for a few nights.

The surroundings around the Piazza were distantly familiar to all, they blended in the best they could. After wandering a while, they went back to the Inn for diner. A 'home stile' setting, they were given large plates of veggies,

Lamb is what came to mind for the protean for everybody. All the other condiments, bread, olive oil and wine were also brought out.

Qwe, "This will surpass beef jerky and biscuit,"

[in English and a quiet voice] All settled in to enjoying the evening. Rym, Mera, Qwe and Tayas were absently listening to all the talk, Rym detected French being spoken over by the fire, a rough looking man he was determined to meet. After finishing, the others had taken to the piazza for a walk, Rym settled himself standing next to the fire, content to listen.

The man was talking to one other his group, that person would translate to Latin. Seems he had sailed from Athens, and the ship was on political visit. The Man did tell of an ambassador on the ship, but mostly just talk of trade. Apparently, the man was more or less a slave, one of the rowing crew, rough looking but seemingly agreeable.

Rym asked what part of France he was from, with a little sideways look, he slowly volunteered,

'Nice' (the location it would be today)

Rym quickly said, "We are just here from Paris, I wanted to know if there is a big market day soon?"

"You are in good time. Tomorrow by the Colosseum"

Rym "Can I fill your cups?"

The three men agreed to that, when Rym returned with the maid following with his offerings. The sailor, not used to being asked for any favor,

"What do you seek?"

Rym "I have a letter and a gift for family members." (He was expanding the truth)

"What be his name"

Rym "Two daughters, their names are Carisa and Lyka Rtyuiop"

"I know not of that names, but tell me of Paris, my brother lives there, does the city grow still?"

Rym "I think it will never stop. All things are in order, at least, for a time, less fighting."

"My friends were telling me just now, more trade is talked of with the Far East, and more trouble with the Ottomans in-between."

He stayed for a short time until talk started to trail off, Rym bid them till tomorrow, another sailor said in passing, "Don't forget the large feast on the hill... food and women! "

Rym tried to sound very interested, but his thoughts were elsewhere.

Finding all sitting around the fountain on a warm
Mediterranean evening, the clear sky seemed to be a novelty to
them all, so very clear, with stars wanting to be touched. Rym filled
them in on the encounter, suggesting they go to the Colosseum
tomorrow, only 1.5 km away, walking the square one more time,
then to their rooms for the night.

Finding the Sleeping bunks not at all comfortable, they all
collected early the next morning in the commons and found it alive
with people talking of the event of the day.

Not sure of the best route, so, when in Roman, do as the
Romans do, and they did.

They accompanied the crowd with people bringing so
many kinds of different wears to sell or trade at the market.

Tayas was commenting how strangely distinctive the
Coliseum looked. All around the grounds the limestone and marble
appeared almost white.

Qwe "It's because it hasn't broken apart yet. Hay, I am
going to tell the future!"

Tayas "Too much Sun already my darling husband?"

Qwe "Au…No…I'm a profit, that will be it! Parts of The
Colosseum will collapse in 1340 something…. Maybe I can sell
tickets!"

Rym "And maybe you will be invited in freely as one of the
400,000 that gave up their last performance here!"

That seemed to put a large lid on his enthusiasm.

Shops all around the perimeter with small coverlets with a thin
canvas make-up, each market stall roof that was held up with long
sticks.

Qwe & Tayas had an interest to see inside, staying close to
where they entered. Rym & Mera said they would be along shortly,
thinking to mingle in the crowd and listen in kind to the locals.

While admiring the interior, Tayas absently asked Qwe, "How am I suppose-to 'see' them, almost all the women have their face covered, and most are older."

Qwe "There is that; I wonder where the Governors meet, I forgot to ask Merlin if she will frequent the outings of the royal court. You know, let's move closer to that large group, I have the translator on, see if we can pick-up some word."

The group appeared to debate something, listing …

"The republic has been split, some good royals, senators and craftsman have been taken south, they want to build a new state center, we cannot let that happen!"

Another voice,

"This is true, we talk to long about it. I will go see one of the generals I know, we have the men, and we have the ships!"

The group seemed very loud, passionate about their cause. Qwe, passing on, wasn't in the market to start a war, only to find his daughters.

Moving back to where Tayas & Qwe were sitting, Rym & Mera slowly meandered up.

Rym "Any useable news?"

Qwe "All we have is the start of what sounds like another war, very glad I don't live here now."

Mera half joking "Yes… we've got you beat! We found a good price on feta cheese and baguettes, holding them out for display, but nothing more, like sum?

Tayas "Yeah, we could use a small bite."

Qwe, do you think you could be careful enough with some pictures, my museum would appreciate it. Don't know how I'll explain it, but I'll manage."

"I can and will, let's walk on a bit."

Having this chance to stroll in ancient history was without question, hard to get used too.

Rym was moving closer to another loud group, listing understanding some talk, really not paying close attention until he thought he heard something.

He grabbed Qwe's arm, "Come listen!"

Turning back to the speaker, Rym pushed Qwe into the crowd, Qwe not knowing what to listen for, following the translator heard the name 'Rtyuiop' and froze, listening for 3-4 minutes. Withdrawing from the group and walking a little off from other people and stopped.

"It really sounded a lot like your last name Rym, it was said a number of times.

He stated that part of the 'High' house had been abducted, a lot of talk about a city in Sicily after that, talk of a battle that was it, Rym this is a clue we can't pass up!"

Tayas, looking at her dad,

Rym "Please understand, I know it's your daughter, but it my granddaughter. We can't act on anything yet; we must return and organize. We don't have enough money for passage to someplace we don't know anything about yet."

Tayas very reluctantly, sadly understood, so did Qwe.

Rym "Tomorrow let's do some research into transportation, for now, let's enjoy right here and now. This all will aid us in our next endeavor to locate the girls."

With the evening descending along with their hopes, they found themselves back at the Inn. Rym thinking historically, the relationships between the two neighboring land masses has been more or less favorable for many long years. They needed more information, hoping to find another person with similar language skills, he moved about the piazza close to the Inn. In truth he found there were 3 groups, pausing at the first listing.

"This is but a small army, with an insane outsider, he is not even Italian! There is no general to oppose him down there, we have a duty!"

Rym passed on to another group, that one seamed to volatile. A smaller number of people here, Rym listened, the next group was speaking French…

"Where did all the money come from for this man, why did they take part of our high house, where did all the ships come from?"

Rym feeling confident spoke up,

"Does anybody know this person's name?"

Lots of men in the crowd volunteered

" Fidalac ... nobody knows where he comes from."

Rym, had an idea and hoped it would work,

"I think I do; he is from a land not easy to find, I hope to be traveling there very soon, I have heard that name, I will try to find him"

Very surprisingly Rym had three people that said they would come with him right now, didn't expect that! He did say he would be back here in 3 weeks, and if possible, would find them. Asking their names, without question they eagerly gave him. These fellows had the look of fighting men, honest, not with sideways glances, shifting eyes, he mused middle of the rough road type that would have to suit him.

Rym would soon learn they were mercenaries.

Around their diner table that evening, the very same was served as the night before, Tayas's thoughts were of course around her girls, what if it could be true? Rym was letting Qwe know what transpired, also an odd question for the first time, asking Qwe how comfortable he is with the saber,

'Very"

Was his only word.

Chapter Twenty-two

Regarding their next trip, Tayas was sensibly discussing funding with Mira. She asked how the museum was able to part with the considerable amount of money, considering the coinage they had here.

"The amount of this vintage of currency is amazing. Bronze, bullion- with copper and silver. They were, of course, salvaged from ships that went down during different wars or storms. We have barrels full, to answer your question."

Tayas "Does the museum have any gold coins, just thinking of fewer coins less weight."

"At that time gold was minted, but for our purposes, we will use what the museum has to offer and still be richer than 97% of Rome!"

The four were enjoying walking the square on another just right Mediterranean evening, talking about all the events that have happened in so short a time.

Qwe was discussing with Tayas about including Tamra on the next trip, saying she could be another pair of eyes in the search. He also mentioned some kind of locating devices for each of them or small walkie-talkies, something to think about.

After a morning coffee type drink, which was kinda roughty tasting, a walk down along the riverfront to reference what might be available for a future sailing trip. Qwe had sailed quite extensively as a young adult and liked to navigate.

Rym with a little background himself, they both really were unsure of a lot of details regarding how they were going to get there.

Observing river skiffs and barges they decided they should be down on the Mediterranean to see what type of ships are indeed available there. Qwe knew from what they found here; this was not the place to start planning an open ocean trip. He volunteered to dive into the research about it when they got back to Geneva.

A slightly cloudy Roman early afternoon was heading their way, knowing their departure time was getting on, they moved over to their transfer point by the stream. It seemed that it was just a small tributary of the Tiber River.

They found that they had company by the creek, two ladies were washing their clothes close to the exit point. They had two hours to wait, so patiently biding their time, they waited. Tayas was on the verge of helping the two ladies when they started packing their baskets, then going up higher on the bank. Up there, the grass was taller to spread the clothes to dry, and away from the thorny bushes here along the stream.

The immediate surroundings seemed to be clear of people, so while waiting for the transfer, Qwe was picking up mid-sized rocks.

Tayas "Samples for study?"

Qwe "No, in-case the tag along ass tries to jump in from the bushes here, I agree with Mera, A bad sort."

At the time the others were lined up on the shore, Qwe was closest to the overgrowth, they started to feel the transfer start...

"Yep... That ass-bite!"

Qwe had five rocks on his arm and was throwing them as they started the transfer, he had four direct hits as Anthony tried to get closer.

One hit at the side of his head which gave him pause. Qwe noticed him caring a large bag, seemingly heavy and he was trying to get what looked like a weapon out! Things quickly phased out, then fading into back into life in Switzerland.

This welcome was a little different, Tamra was with Dr. J and more than a little worried, looking at Tayas & Qwe,

Tamra "I am going next time! You drove me nuts!"
Rym was next to tell Qwe,

"Good exercise, glad you got rid of Anthony! I hadn't taken that idea that far ahead!"

Qwe coming to his senses sounded very worried

"Did you see him trying to pull a gun out!"

All the others hadn't, and it stopped everyone cold!

Qwe "It looked like it was a type of gun that is manufactured now in this time!"

Rym "Well this puts aside mark on our approach to traveling! We now have to make ourselves a little more secure somehow! To my knowledge, none of our group knows anything about guns, or a very little, am I correct?"

Everybody did concur except Tamra,
"I know two someone's who love that stuff…"

Tayas "Who two are you thinking about?"

Tamra "Ozbetin and Art."

Qwe "I hope they like to travel."

The appointed leader of this group seems to always get the last information and outdated news. Dr. Johnstone is invaluable to the flow of everything. Somebody must have the wherewithal to contrive reasons for the travelers when they don't arrive back on time at their regular jobs.

The config's first direction involved Anthony, who, why and what was his intention, who was he involved with?

Everything about this project was so new, there was no historical background of their own for any reasonable reference. To remedy that, they decided after each phasing event, they would establish a ritual. In a quiet room, each one would record all the facts they could individually remember. It took extra time, but somewhere along the way, it could be of great benefit.

Tamra again stayed overnight with Tayas & Qwe. She needed the two of them to let things out, it was decided everyone should take a day off.

The next sunny morning found Qwe with maps, and Tayas with her tablet uncovering any and all they could regarding transportation available in the day. Tamra was also studying Sicily, Palermo in particular. Historically around the time they were present, she had discovered a few medium skirmishes with Rome, and the Ottomans, eventually settling into all things Rome of course.

Tayas, reminding them about the idea of some type of protection, and asked if they should bring something along.

Each one had decided to take a class and familiarize themselves with handling different kinds of guns or devices. It was decided it would be brought up again when everybody was together.

Mera was getting in touch with the staff she was affiliated with at the museum, regarding the period of the coin that she needed for the next adventure. The staff had an interest in what Mera intended the use of the coinage. Her very casual return was,

"A large-scale reenactment of History," which wasn't too much of a departure from the truth.

The following Monday morning Rym & Dr. J were right into it again,

"Here we have a crystal from Alva glen, one from Rome and one from nobody knows where.

A possible destination was given to us by Merlin, a distant universe and a distant time plus or minus infinity..."

Dr. J had assessed the unknown crystal with all of the same light spectrum and lazier analysis and was pressing Rym to undertake a single 2-hour trip.

The thought was only for the identification of the period, just a small trip without company.

Rym understanding it must be done at some time had to agree.

This was Wednesday, Friday was the next Hadron Collider run with multiple times, so with a deep exhale of breath, it was decided.

Not knowing again where and when he might land, he dressed as of today, and took a change for past. Dr. J giving Dr. Rym the printed Collider schedule, then wishing him the best. The high humming and vibrating feeling - phasing of the transfer started to blur, then phasing back to normal, all was well and done on the Geneva side of things.

Chapter Twenty-three

Dr. Rym slowly addressing his new circumstance, he found himself in a small dome shaped room with a sizable offering of crystals, methodically placed on shelves. Amazed, he noticed each one had a tag and number. In his curiosity to see more of the surrounding building, he headed for the only oval-shaped door and found himself in a small foyer, with five oval hallways branching off.

The surrounding building walls were smooth and lightly colored, some paved with what looked like semi-rough plastic, one of the walkways was just dirt.

No sound, just a smell of new electrical wire hit his senses, not unpleasant but odd.

Picking the hall that he felt a slight air current issuing from, started off checking his watch. Placing a crystal on the floor from the transfer room to mark his choice of exit. Giving some thought to the possibilities of time open to him for return, he had to head back to Switzerland in one hour or in three.

Taking in more of his new surroundings, the lighting of the interior was ample from room to hall, but he didn't note any light switches or light fixtures. He was a little concerned about people meeting him here and how to justify his presents.

Slowly, quietly following still the same hall which now opened into a sizable, tiered lecture hall, on the far side he took notice of some glass doors and outside natural light.

Moving in that direction still not seeing anyone, found the oval doors with no locks or didn't appear to have any, and passed easily through.

Taking one step outside he stopped mid-stride, trying to take in this extraordinarily fantastic world he had been unknowingly introduced into!

Lavish welcoming gardens everywhere, while overhead there were floating buildings of massive proportions. Floating transports of varying size and shape left him speechless!

Slowly walking on very manicured pathways, he heard a person (he thought) singing in a language that Rym had no inkling of.

Not wanting to be found out, he moved away from the path and into bushes & trees, everything was immaculate. Staying still himself, he watched the man pass and noticed the man was soliloquizing to a hologram issuing from his outstretched hand! Then out into a walkway that leads around a small lake, or what appeared to be, or possibly a large slow-moving picture of water!

There were no cars; animals, motor-driven anything on the ground. Coming up carefully to the 'street' five or six more people, who were talking in groups, none seemed to take notice of him.

Feeling less of a public target, he moved down the street watching the people, turning slowly around he walked right into a woman as she came around a corner.

Rym naturally responded "Au… pardon me!"

The woman looked mildly confused. She started speaking in a language that Rym, had no knowledge of. Next, trying to communicate with hand signals, Rym noticed her pointing at her waist, at some buttons on her coat. Of course, Rym shrugging his shoulders as if to say,

'I don't understand.'

She motioned for him to follow. With nothing else to go on, he followed along, and what the heck!

Following her along the path, they very soon passed into what appeared to be a small food court.

She stopped front of a small kiosk and pushed a bank of buttons, and a jacket appeared on a hanger, pointing at Rym then at herself, he put the coat on. Then she said something; still he didn't understand, she stated again, looking at his mouth and speaking. Rym understood,

"I am sorry I bumped into you."

Nothing happened.

She pressed a certain location on his jacket, he tried again,

Rym "I did not intend to bump into you…"

123

"There we are, did you leave your coat at home?"

Rym thinking, "No, you are very kind, I am new here, didn't know where things were."

"I can tell you're not from this here and now, you are dressed very differently."

Rym, to make certain,

"Yes quiet, I cannot pay you for this jacket…"

"They are of no value; all peoples have one type of them due to all the many languages from different Galaxies that come to our world. Would you like to dress yourself with something more suitable?''

Rym "Yes, if I may."

"Follow me."

Stepping to the other side of the pavilion

"Remove the jacket and things of value, then step in there."

Gesturing Rym into a changing room, but was again unsure,

"I cannot pay for this and I…."

"Really, it is of no consequence, I will be here waiting." She pressed six buttons and flash… No more than 30 sec. later, his new casual day ware slid down a shoot.

Now feeling and looking like he lived here, stepping out, rearranged his daypack she asked

"Where would you like to go?"

Rym was mildly startled, looking at his watch

"Well, I must be back here in one hour, but first, let me introduce myself, my name is Rym."

"I seem to be in not much of a hurry myself, my name is Emily."

Rym " I have never been here before, possibly you could tell me what I should see."

Emily with a smile,

"All right, I think a 30-minute tour will do."

Rym "I can't take you from what you were doing!"

Emily "Doing? Nobody does much doing here…."

"Then you are very kind, your husband will be expecting you."

"No husband, my partner, who I will be meeting here in 3 hours. We will be dinning and watching the sunset; you are welcome to come with us."

Rym, again very surprised
"Thank-you, I will try and arrange it."

Emily "Lets tour."

Moving outside of the pavilion not very far at all, they stepped onto a moving sidewalk that took them too an underground terminal.

There she chose a car with 4 individual seats, stepping right in, she pushed a formula of buttons, and for a time they traveled underground. Outside away from the buildings, she started to explain what this and that was.

Rym observed no track or roads that they were moving on, and really didn't care, he now realized they were floating! Everywhere! No noise, very smooth and calm, after 25 minutes she brought him back to the Plaza they started from.

Rym was discreetly planning he would return back to Switzerland, hopefully find Mera, then return here. He composed his agenda quickly, telling her he had to go on a small trip.

So, asking where they would be in 1.5 hrs., he will try to be back here then. She stated they would be in this general vicinity.

Ok, ok… thinking to himself as he quickly headed back to the garden, through the ovel doors to the hall, back to the crystal phasing room. With 10 min to spare before the next travel time, he was thinking about Mera, he could call ASAP when back. Waiting for a few minutes, then phasing, gone- and -back at the laboratory in Switzerland.

Dr. J was admiring his clothes while Rym went for the phone.

"Well, when or what are we looking at do you know…?"

Rym "Not now Dr. I need Mera! (calling) Yes, are you still here? Must come here! Fast…. Dr. J when is the next test? Change that! What are the times for all tests!"

He started to hurriedly re-packing things into another daypack, talking over his shoulder,

"I don't know what year but it's far in the future, and…"

Mera actually came running in…

"Where are we going?"

Rym "How did ya know?"

"Is the dress like that?" pointing at him.

"Yes"

She had left her old pack here and was going through it, "Nothing… I have some other things over in my office…"

Rym "No, your fine now, I can get you changed in 5 mins out there…"

Looking at Dr. J still talking and assuming,

"1,3,5 nights."

Rym still running with Mera all over trying to get settled.

Rym "When is the next transit Dr.?"

"8 mins and 49 seconds."

Rym "Mera, we are watching the sunset and having dinner tonight with two very nice lesbians, or at least one is nice."

A busy silence as everybody still re-packing,

Mera "Boy, it took days to get any information on our last trip, you go out for one hour, and we're almost moving there!"

Dr. J. Handing the latest printout to each of them.

Rym, "I know one night at least… Three most likely, there doesn't seem to be a need for money, as far as I know, we will find out. I know Tayas & Qwe, and of course our dear Tamra will want to know."

Mera "Please make our excuses Dr. J."

Dr. J "As always…"

Standing in their launch & retrieve site "Ready Mera? "

Mera with an adventurous smile,

"Your kinda fun…. yes."

phase…tuning back in slowly, this place in time was all new for Mera, Rym had hoped they brought all of what they needed.

Taking a breath and stepping out, they moved along the halls to the garden.

Mera with a gasp "There's no lack of imagination here!" Walking out along the same route that Rym had recently been on, he was hoping that he could get the machines to work. At the jacket kiosk, he gave it a try and didn't have a problem, two buttons pictures of M/F. That was easy, now over to the other synthesizer,

hmm… 6 buttons and the images were not so very self-explanatory.

As they both were studying the instruction panel, there was a familiar voice behind Rym,

"Hello, again Rym."
Rym turned, reassured and smiling

"Yes, hello, I must apologize, Emily, I am helping myself hopefully with your permission. Let me introduce Mera, I wanted to bring her along."

"How do you do, my name is Emily… Mera, how would you like to enjoy some of the finest and latest in fashion?"

Said very sarcastically,

"I'm in need it does appear, and would like to blend in a little better, thank you, Emily."

As the ladies dressed, Rym was taking pictures of the new surroundings, some minutes later, the ladies stepped out,

Rym "You ware it just so Mera!"

"Thanks to Emily"

Rym "I must apologize, for our tardiness, and for inviting Mera without asking"

Emily "Rym, first I must be the one to…. (Catching sight of Lisa) Hay Lisa! Over here…!"

Lisa approaching the group,

"What have you come up with Emily, a surprise party! All these nice people and I thought you had forgotten my birthday!"

Emily "Yep, that's what I did, well this will be like a birthday surprise after I let you know what we have the start of!"

"Sounds intriguing, let's get on the way, my name's Lisa." Intros and they all jumped into a floating car that whisked them over to the Coast.

Their location was perfect, on the top row all around view of a semi cloudy Sunset with warm layered colors. Everybody settling in with some lesser talk, Emily wanted to engage Rym again,

"As I have been trying to say all afternoon, it is I that should apologize. I was the instigator of our collision earlier, I 'saw' your gift."

That comment brought Mera around to look closer at Rym and with several surprises

"Oh my, you do! I must be honest; I was looking for something else and I..."

Rym, wanting to save her some embarrassment, "Maybe it was the same thing I was looking for in you?"

Expressive smiles appeared on their faces. Letting that issue drop for a while, Rym felt compelled to give their hostesses an idea why they both have found themselves here.

"We are in an anxious search for my granddaughters, and new to phasing. We have no clues as to their where-about, so we are at very best, randomly trying to locate them somewhere in this vast Universe."

Emily "We also have phasing available to us as you know Dr., but we rarely bother with it. Most people use it for amusement, a week here or there at most. All of us have gotten very used to living at the point of a button or a thought, so it's not thought of or used much.

An acquittance of ours let us know about some gifted travelers that we would be meeting, and now you are here. What are your granddaughter's names?"

Rym "Lyka and Carisa-Uisge Rtyuiop, they were taken at three years of age, we have found one. Still, we are following any ideas."

Lisa "Uisge-That's Gaelic for liquid, Carisa could maybe on one of the water planets?"

Emily "That's an idea, how long will you be staying?"

Rym "We leave tomorrow mid-morning, and that is another thought, we need to find a place for the night."

Emily, "No, we need you to stay with us. There are so many things we must decipher together, is it possible to stay longer here?"

Mera, "We could, let's take a look."
Rym was already getting out the printout, unfolding it….

Lisa was amused pointing,

"Look Emily, how quaint, paper!"

Rym smiling,

"I am sure this is quite different here."

At that, she pressed an inside pad on her coat, and a three-D Tablet appeared floating 2 feet in front of her

"You also have this available, press inside left collar and speak what you want to be remembered."

Mera had pushed a wrong location, but Emily corrected her,

Mera "That is perfect… I could use this at home!"

Emily "You may, but it would be problematic. If you were to be found out, it would cause much trouble."

Rym, "These are not dependent on a host-based device?"

Emily "No, they are autonomous. What's your schedule like?"

Rym, "We could stay two more nights after tonight if that's inconvenient we will leave tomorrow."

Emily "Stay longer, we've an important number of places we must visit, and a few people to see, ok: I 'm ready for dinner, anybody?"

Chapter Twenty-four

Qwe & Tayas and Tamra, here at home, wanted to know the latest from Dr. J and why Rym's exit was in so much haste.

"I am going to be of little help to you three because it was just that. As Rym was calling Mera and gathering things, he said he was going to watch the sunset, didn't say where. Oh yes, he did say lesbians, yes, he did mention two lesbians, and he was wearing some futuristic clothes of some sort."

Tamra, standing comfortably with fingers in her pants pockets,

"My-my, how very enlightened grandpop is for a 12 Th century King to be so worldly and excepting…"

Tayas, "Was he concerned, worried or anything of that nature?"

Dr. J "No, just worried Mera wasn't going to get here in time."

Qwe, "They agreed on one or three nights?"

"Rym did mention three so, probably thus, he almost seemed happy!"

Tamra, "I think I would also be; they maybe float there, just think…"

Tayas, "This is serious!"

"Oh mom, just having a little fun, Oz and I had…"

"Stop!" … Tayas staring,

Qwe, "I think we still should keep planning on the…well, hold on, [stepping to the white board] I'll say Terra -1, our first quest, was for Tamra, our second, will be Alva glen, Sterling and the third will be Rome and forth will be the future"

diagraming it all, T-1, -2, T-3, T-4, T-5, etcetera……….

"All right, Rym & Mera in T-4 now, let's keep at planning for the return to T-3, Should we include a possibility of going to Palermo?

We only heard that possibility once, and if we do, sailing would be easiest. It's 427 km, better than on a horse-drawn cart, it would cost less and easier on ourselves.

Speaking of the money question, Dr. J what are they using for money wherever they are now?"

"Rym told Mera they didn't need money there."
Tayas & Tamra looked at each other shocked!

Qwe "Well, we're going to need coinage in Rome, we will ask when they return, Dr. J an idea came to us on the issue of including self-protection, if it is too be a longer stay, what are your thoughts."

"Let's see how many there will be... Rym, Tayas, Qwe, not Tamra..." at that, she jumped in

"I am too! ... pardon me, Dr. J."

"You remember what the wishes of Merlin were, that you be protected, he may be very true."

"I know, but I can't take it here when they are gone, you know how I was bugging you, right Dr.?"

"Yes, yes I will leave that to your mom & dad.... As far as the gun issue is concerned, you all must know that if it were found out, all history would be changed. Along with the cameras and individual locators you plan on taking. You all would be thrown in jail! ... At best! But I also see the need for a small group too have protection, let's open this discussion again when all are present."

Qwe "Let's do that Dr. How do the test schedules look, for all we know we could be gone for a month or so, if we must go to Palermo then back to Rome? Sailing back then was a lot slower than today."

Dr. J "I am thinking for that amount of time hum.... We are going to need to invent some kind of marker to be sent back and forth. It should blend in to look compatible with its surroundings and be able to leave itself in the middle of a room it lands in, or on the bank of a river. I will manufacture something. For now, the startup schedules are at the longest one month out. I will think about this."

Qwe "Tamra, I was wondering how you would feel if it was that long? You have experienced what it is like, major camping out at times."

Tamra "I am still intent on going, but I'll really review myself and consider everything.''

Tayas, "That's the first time in a long time I have heard you sound serious!"

Tamra "Just thinking about Oz."

Tayas "Ah ha, that's the reason!"

"Well, Mother...aumm, I kinda like him, and you know…" Qwe was thoughtfully listening, thinking…

"What if you were to ask him to come with us?"

Tayas & Tamra together turned and spoke

"What is that about?"

Qwe "I am starting to look at it as a long-term trip and how it would appear in our travels, possibly for all of us to have partners.

In the event, and I hope it doesn't happen, if we do need to defend ourselves, we have men to answer with. And you already mentioned Tamra, that Oz knows a lot about weapons, he and Atriums go hunting and shooting range together a lot apparently."

Tamra was amusingly surprised into thinking,

"That would be cool…. yeah, he and Art, fish and hunt, they know about all that gun stuff, hmm…"

Qwe "How do you think they would handle the long travel; you know we haft a keep all this very quiet…"

Tamra "Dad, they think their James Bonds brother, so no problem. Oz is here at work, you want ta ask him now, or I can ask later?"

Qwe, "Yes, with most of our group here, I think so yes."

Tamra "I'll go get him, fill him in along the way, phuee! Now I can tell him I talked with Merlin!"

Qwe & Tayas together, "Quietly!" (let's follow along with Tamra for some other amusement…)

Oz works around the Collider 5 minutes away, and so she called first to get him out of his lab & up at the receptionist.

Seeing him, she sauntered up,

"Hi!" grabbing his lab coat sleeve and playfully dragging him outside, stopping under an eve, then looking square in his face…

"How would you like to travel back in time, check out Rome when it was sort-a new, meet all kinds of different people. Then sail to Sicily in a small boat, rescue a Princess, and then bring her back here…

Oh, yeah… You have to Kick all kinds of butt and shoot ugly bad guys."

This all was happened really fast for Oz. Hosting a very puzzled look,

"What the hell are you talking about?"

Impatiently, Tamra with a glaring look,

"Bite me! I really mean what I'm talking about!"

Oz, reaching for her with a mischief's smile,

"Actually, I wouldn't mind biting you…"

She lightly smacked him, grabbing his lab coat and tugging him around a corner, she noticed a soda bottle in the bushes, bringing him to a stop.

Pointing a focused finger, picking-up the bottle and levitated it to him.

Oz "How did… You made… the bottle. It flew!"

She then grabbed him by his coat lapels and kissed him,

"How did that feel to kiss a real Princess!"

With all her attitude showing, she turned to purposely walk away, he slowly followed, while starting to paint a mental picture of adventure, he gradually came around,

Tamra still walking without turning, over her shoulder,

"Interested?"

Oz was running now,

"Can you do that again?"

"Sure!"

She stopped, turned and kissed him again, turned and walked…

"Well, I meant the floaty flying thing!"

"Not here, there's all kinds of people around now, get a grip! Follow me…."

In came the new recruit still trailing Tamra, approaching everyone,

"He's in."

With that quickly accomplished, Qwe started giving Oz a little background.

The other Dr's were catching up on other tests and research that they had put off for quite some time. As the days passed by, Oz became very familiar with what the enterprise was attempting to undertake. Without any doubt the others were more than pleased with the addition.

Tamra, of course was quietly thrilled that Oz wanted to follow her along into Time.

Chapter Twenty-five

Rym & Mera woke-up floating!

"That is without a doubt the best night I have ever had!"

Mera, "I didn't feel my back at all this morning! Just right in every place. And I must say, my best too!"

Emily & Lisa sitting in their 'kitchen' welcomed the two,

"All the stuff around here is like last night, so help yourself, just ask for it."

Mera, "Cappuccino…. Two Please"

Soon after a tray floated out of a space in the wall settling on the table. Both the newcomers marveled still at all the automation and conveniences here at home and out in public.

Emily "I would like to introduce you to a person here that will help us, then out to the coast for a meeting before lunch, if that is ok. Lisa has other people to get in touch with regarding you both."

Their hosts had mentioned a clairvoyant: 'Paul,' was the name, he was to be the first for this morning. Rym & Mera still getting used to floating buildings, the transport and finding it captivating. Freeways here didn't have solid sub-straight, just cars that seemed to go where they wanted to go, and it always appeared that they were the only ones in the air.

Rym later found out, all the others were invisible to them as they were invisible to everybody else.

Automatically dropping them off at the address, and being issued in to see Paul, in a building 15 levels high, with a 180° view.

Emily introduced them all and wanted to express the importance of Rym & Mera's arrival.

Paul started right in

"What you know and have been told is very important but what you are about to learn will be of the highest value, and will be a possibility, difficult to digest. I am gifted with seeing into the future, Emily has told me of 'Carisa Rtyuiop' who you have been looking for, I know not of her yet.

I say yet because I resolve myself to find her. She is not here in this world; I have sent runners to other planets for a search."

"Rym & Mera you have recently talked with 'Merlin of old.'

What you now must understand is, we are trying extremely hard to stop other worlds from taking 'Gifts' from his world and acquiring vast sums of (we would call it money) tangibles and unfortunately, humans. They are sold as the buyers believing they have many gifts, in truth, only a select few have gifts and none are not treated humanely.

We have an individual who calls himself ' Fidalac ' thinks of himself as a maker of people, a maker of history. He is delusional on the very smallest level, but in moving people on other worlds at the right time, unfortunately, does change things on other planets and this one as well. A simple corresponding illustration would be to refer to a game of three dementia chess, but on a planetary scale."

Mera, "Seeing things from the past, is it possible to acquire Rym's granddaughters and make a change that would force that incident from not happening?"

"No, we cannot go back and re-establish events or the original family.

Far too much would change with other Earth histories. Yes, there will be war again, that takes place at its source, Merlin's world."

Mera, "That is my home-world, can the war be taken to this other man's world?"

"No, magic must win back the day! It must consume those that profit from the export of it."

Rym, "Does this endanger my granddaughters?"

"Details are hard to 'see' in the future of the past at great lengths or the past only present and past, 100 years on each side. Mera, you are one with gifts, you must be cautious, your company's success will depend mostly on Tamra's presence. I know this from past encounters.

My 'runners' are not as centrally focused as I am, so finding Carisa will be an investment with time."

Starting to stand, no handshakes,

Paul "Thank-you for coming, Rym & Mera we will talk again."

On their way to the Coast, Mera had more thoughts as well as Rym, Emily was answering questions on money, or the lack of it here.

"We all have work cycles 1 year on, 2 years off. We gave up printing money because it was too expensive, the reason it worked when you purchased Mera's coat was the proximity of your old jacket to the machine."

Rym, "We must financially help somehow!"

Emily "Do believe me, they cost next to nothing."

Taking in the view outside passing by trees and all the landscape looked groomed, their altitude was at about 155 m and quickly made the coast.

The extraordinary geological features, arches, white beaches, and purplish-blue rock sea cliffs.

Emily talking over things at lunch, was asking Rym if they would meet with two others tomorrow,

"You do have one full day after today I didn't want to crowd today."

Rym "That suits me, Mera how about you?"

Mera "You both, have been very kind, that sounds fine with me. The two of us wanted to ask about an event that happened on one of our transfers back from Merlin's world. We were just starting when a man, literally jumped out of the bushes and transferred back with us to our lab. We did take him back to Rome his home, but he tried again, when we were leaving, this time he tried to draw a gun manufactured in our day and age."

Lisa & Emily had very concerned expressions,

Emily "What did that person look like?"

Rym "Dressed in cloths of the time, thin, black hair, average height, he spoke Greek and Latin."

Lisa "That could be Anthony ..."

Mera, "Yes, that's the name he gave us, I had an issue of trust, that I brought up with Rym."

Emily "He speaks many languages; he is a lieutenant for Fidalac who Paul referred to as deranged. How long did he stay in your time?"

"Just two nights, we didn't let him out of the laboratory and was under the observation of my colleague the entire time we were gone."

Emily "This change lots of things, I'll call Paul, Lisa would you call your two gentlemen and update them, we'll step into a privet room to make our calls, be right back,"

Leaving the couple to sip some refreshment and enjoy the layered late afternoon sky.

Chapter Twenty-six

Late afternoon lake rain persisted here in Geneva, the general groundwork had been arranged for the next trip, they now needed to get Rym & Mera back here to confirm a few things. Today at 2:00 is their arrival time, the Collider spooled up on que, the pleasing hum/vibe blurry fuzz started to appear, then focus and back too this Earth, whole again.

Tamra was the first to greet the new comers,

"Hi grand pop, how was the trip? Guess what, Oz is coming with us! Oh, and Art to!"

Rym, "Slow up young lady, we just got back granddaughter!"

All smiles, hugs.

With the evening coming on and conversion still running substantially high, the recent travelers called it a night. Leaving Dr. J to pour over much of what was just gleaned from Rym & Mera.

Chapter Twenty-seven

Tayas was unconsciously making hast, motherhood was internally manifesting itself. Qwe was feeling the same underlying current of a father with subtle outward sign. They needed to find their girls.

On the other hand, Tamra had issues, and with no uncertain terms would leave it to chance to let everybody know about it,

"Hay, you know what Oz said, we have to 'ugly ourselves up a lot <u>more</u>!' And he was talking about me & you mom! more...?"

Said with a foot stomp and her arms folded!

Atriums "You really stepped into that one Oz."

Oz "Now, you know I didn't say it like that, I said that you were so pretty, like your mom. I thought a disguise would be a good idea. People at that time were mostly <u>hideous</u>, they would think something was up!"

Qwe, coming to his rescue,

"I think he has a valid concern, we must fit in, we all could use smuggled faces, we might have an extended stay."

Along the following week and a half, Mera had located the dated coins needed for the trip, along with maps and sea charts of the time at her museum .

Rym was brushing up on the vernacular of the day, (Latin) Qwe decided to rely on his solar translator, was sewing the earpieces into his tattered overcoat.

Mera had to remind Tamra that they could buy things they all needed when the right time approached.

Dr. J & Rym were discussing the Collider event scheduled, also was going over a device that they could send back and forth, what Dr. J came up with was a thick gelatin covering a hollow fiberglass rock.

Only handwritten notes, a recording device wouldn't work due to the gelation was too obscure for solar recharge.

Dr. J "The gelatin seems to act as skin, and hollow rock seems to respond as a body would. I have sent this to Alva glen and back with success."

Rym, "This I don't think would work in the crystal room, it would appear too obvious."

"Yes, I am aware of that and will address that when needed."

Chapter Twenty-eight

With all in attendance and ready for Rome, their next destination, Tamra was explaining to Oz,

"You don't haft 'a be nervous, it's a real nice hmmm, then everything vibes a little then goes out of focus, then back in focus."

Oz, "Thanks Tamra, but remember, Art and I like new adventures, I'm feeling very comfortable."

Art "Let's go find those sisters of yours!"

So, off to Rome they went, sometime in the 12 Th. century. Fading in by the little stream again, with clear skies and a beautiful warm Roman afternoon. Rym & Qwe started off in the direction of the Inn they had stayed at before, in hopes of meeting the four sailors again. Tamra was playing the role of tour guide,

"Check out the houses, now and kinda down over that way is the Coliseum, and oh yea, we are crossing over the Tiber River."

Tayas, quietly admonishing Tamra

"No English Tamra, please."

Oz in French with a smile, "Thanks Tamra, you wonderful goofball, we were just here with Athena some weeks ago at my Uncles Villa, and don't forget, this isn't that far from Geneva."

Tamra "Yes but you weren't here in the 12th century!"

Oz "That's very true, the buildings are a tad shorter and not quite so many but look about the same, oh, by the way, you still look pretty even with mud on your face."

Tamra "Au, you think so?"

Oz "yes."

Atriums discreetly caught Oz's attention and gave him a thumbs up, both smiling....

The Piazza Navona wasn't as crowded, so rooms with a view of the plaza were available. Oz was adjusting quite well, finding some French but mostly Latin was spoken, his not being of much benefit.

Art, on the other hand, knew Latin & Greek from his study in Botany.

Rym wanted to head down to the common room to try to locate the sailors/mercenaries.

The evening was quiet, the stars appeared to sparkle and dance, they found themselves at a table outside, with almost the exact menu items places in front of them. Rym hadn't recognized anybody yet, so after dinner, they strolled the plaza for a small time. Everybody but Rym was for turning in early, so he found a right spot to listen and waited. With little success, he soon also retired for the night.

Friday morning was quite a bit different, the plaza was filling with people, and they appeared to be heading the same way as they had before.

So, when in Rome, do as the Romans do, winding through the narrow-cobbled streets, and finding themselves up again by the Colosseum.

Tamra wanted to check out the inside, Qwe, Tayas, Mera, Rym, and Artemis wanted to mingle. Market days almost everywhere are always filled with very diverse people and languages.

Wandering for hours without seeing or hearing any wanted success, they slowly ambled into the shade, so far at a loss.

 Heading inside where they were met Tamra's excitable voice,

"I heard a group of men discussing the senate, and Dad's name came up!"

Qwe, "Are they still around?"

Tamra "I left Oz there, this way!"

Rounding a corner in a round building, (yes, I did say that...)

Found the men Rym recognized, two of them from their last trip back at the Inn.

Rym approached hopefully and listened, they were still talking about Sicily, Palermo and what this man Fidalac had taken.

Rym wasn't in any place to fund a small army. Nor did he have any background in that field, one of the men remembered Rym and came over and asked if he had any new ideas about this man.

Rym, "None yet, my friend said you mentioned a name 'Rtyuiop,' what story have you of that name?"

"A Princess I am told, and there is a reward given for her and two others, a son of a senator and his wife."

Rym, "The first name of the other prisoner, do you know that?"

"No, we only know the last name 'Rtyuiop,' and they are not at the governors' palace. Somewhere out in the countryside. Do you intend to find them?"

Rym, "Yes, but I cannot pay all these men, we will try ourselves."

"Are you staying at the same Inn as last time?"

Rym "Yes, there are seven of us total, we are going back soon."

Man "I will be there after the sun."

The company sitting at dinner, (of the same) were hopefully optimistic about the information they were going to get. Halfway thru, they were greeted by the man that Rym had met. Inviting him to sit, (For the reader, remember this new man spoke French)

Qwe "We are not interested in any reward, we are interested only in the Princess, is it possible to find this place and safely rescue her? I don't intend or want to storm the place with a large force."

Man "I must agree with you, that's why just I am here. I was a sailor in Palermo for five years. I was born in Paris that's how I speak French. I know the countryside all around Palermo, I have friends there. I must tell you; I kill people for money."

Said in a whisper.

Rym, unfazed, "There is one single thing that must be clear, no harm is to come to her."

Rym speaking in a low clear voice,

"We have no concerns about money, if that does follow, we want nothing to do with it."

"That is good for me, now I must ask, are just the men coming?"

Tayas, "No"
"My thought is how were you going to get there?"

Qwe, "Boat, and it sounds as if we are talking to the right man, I have a lot of experience, but not with your ships of the line here."

Rym, "It is my intention for you to help us getting there, help find the princess, then return here."

"That depends on the reward getting paid. I don't want to waste time on a scenic boat ride."

Rym, "Let's go out around the plaza and settle things, Mera, if you please, I would like your hand in this."

And it was made so, the excitement at the table was raised a few notches, by the time Rym & Mera got back, it was time for another round of wine.

Rym "Our little outing is going to be a long time at sea, I sure hope none of us are prone to seasickness!"

Tamra "Just exactly how long?"
With a downturned face.

Rym, " It's 143 leagues or 427 km. It will take one week to get there…. Does anybody want to stay here?"

Tamra, "You think I'm chicken? You have a lot to learn gramps, I mean Dr., I mean your Majesty, I mean… forget it, of course, I'm still going!"

Tayas, "The ships of the day here are not like the cruisers of our day, dear daughter."

Oz "It's probably a square-rigged something, that is rowed by 20 slaves and stinks like shit!"

Rym smiling "Oz, I think you have a good idea of it."

Qwe "So Dr's, you two have a good feeling about this man?
"

Looking at each other,

Rym, "Good enough, we agreed on a price, and told him we have left, the bulk of his payment here with our 'friends,' that would be his pay off when we get back, oh yes, his name is Max."

Chapter Twenty-nine

Gathering the not so rested company together early the morning, Max informed them they would be riding in a flatbed, horse drawn wagon for a day and a half. First night we will spend at a friend's farmhouse.

The following day we will stay at an Inn the driver knows in 'Fiumicino' the port town.

Tamra had ridden on hayrides when she was a kid, but after twenty minutes the hay padding was flattened, but did the princess complain?

"What the hell is this fucked up bullshit! This is crap! … We need more fat ass hay!"

In a word, "Yes!"

It all was smoothed over with a stop by a vineyard the driver knew, more hay was added, and the Princess was once again appeased.

The first night was had in a comfortable bunkhouse off the main house, the vineyard fieldworkers were put in the barn.

Next day started early, and yes, more hay was added. The balance of the trip was uneventful. Finally, the village and the Mediterranean, with the new profoundly agreeable fragrance of the sea surrounding the company. Surveying the two ships, available for passage, a ten-slave row vessel or a med sized Gaff rigid ship. Rym & Qwe asked Max which he would choose,

"Definitely not the one with all the men, that would do with speed, but would not with the women."

Max walked them to the Inn, Barcelo Aran Blu (in the area of what is now 'Port of Ostia') very close to the harbor. All were looking forward to spending the night on a flat, nonmoving surface.

Max headed off to the Marina to make arrangements for passage as soon as possible.

Mera, Tayas and Tamra, were all comparing bruises and now were joking about their ride. The group was very pleased with what was offered at dinner, two different selections, lamb or fish were provided, almost everybody chooses the flounder.

Max was as kind as he knew how, which isn't saying much, he was trying to explain in detail about their trip.

"You will have an aft cabin to yourselves with eight hammocks. Oatcakes, bread, and water they have. If I were you, I wouldn't let the crew see your dried foodstuffs, keep that amongst yourself in your cabin."

Oz "How long of a trip will it be?"

Max "Less than a week if the wind is kind, we will stay here for two nights while the ship finishes getting fitted-out. Enjoy your time here, it's not so pretty on board."

He left them to see other people he knew.

Mera was starting to wonder of herself adapting to sea life. From the looks of the small boat, the shadows of queasiness seem to be lurking some where in amongst the aging wooden ship.

Still, enjoying their walk along the boardwalk, the warm night, a quartering moon with stars that were winking at you.

Oz had hold of Tamra's hand and mentioned as the others were heading for the Inn, they were going to cruz the boardwalk a little more.

He was concerned that Tamra was going to be very out of sort on the ship.

"I will do anything within my power to keep good care of you, but the smells, and add in the very close quarters, you are kinda on your own."

Tamra "Thanks Oz, you can be a real gentleman when you want, I like it. Don't worry about me so much I am tougher than I look. I play the Princess thing up because I think it's funny, and I know Rym, Tayas, and Qwe are used to it. So, it's my own stretched sense of humor that makes me look fragile ."

Walking, gazing at the night sky reflections on the tranquil water, listening to the softly lapping sea caressing each ship or pilling in their turn. The stars felt like they wanted to be touched, just being together arm in arm without a word, walking in a dream.

[You must keep in mind that you are not on earth as you live it here, this world has most of the same past history that you and I live on. Much of the petty violence does not exist here in other words, it's safe for Oz & Tamra to hang out at the docks after dark.]

Mera, Rym, Tayas and Qwe over the next couple of days all did much of the same. The thought of the departure morning (early) had them all anticipating the adventure with hopeful ideas of what might be, far beyond the tall blue peak of the next wave.

Chapter Thirty

Arriving at dawn, balancing on a very narrow gangplank on to the medium sized sailing ship. Max was showing them to their quarters, helping them stow their bags, explaining where to and where not to go. Tamra was sarcastically surprised to find their cabin was smaller than she expected,

"Ck it out, a window! And these five-star hammock's? Shit!"

With an open look of disgust, she wisely chose not to malign any of the other ships complement, but the ship's Captain was as she did put it,

"A little prick."

Getting underway with the waning tide, with very little wind. The captain set four men to row through the harbor mouth and get them a little on their way. The small ship they were on was named "Fortunam Maris" which translates to "Luck of the Sea"

Tamra had to ask her dad,

"What the hell does that mean, since when has the sea been lucky?"

Qwe "Why don't you ask the little prick?"

Tamra "Ha-ha dad! Now I can appreciate your humor in a totally different light, good one Ha-ha."

The ship was gaff ringed, with a light wind the crew didn't have much to do and was more or less, checking the ladies out.

That was until the captain caught sight of them and got them back to the task. Tamra started to rethink her assessment of him, maybe the captain was a good guy after all.

They would be sailing south on the Tyrrhenian Sea, more or less along the west coast of Italy until Folio Ischia, a small island off Naples, then direct to Palermo.

As the morning started coming up, the wind freshened, and things seemed as they should be. Mera feeling better than expected, as was the whole company. Tayas, Mera and Tamra talking amongst themselves about how much they we're enjoying the first few hours of the trip so far. Then on a side note, Tamra asked where the bathroom was, the men just laughed,

Qwe, "Didn't you notice the bucket by our window in the cabin?"

Tamra "No way! You guys are messin' with me, right?" All in unison with smiles, "No!"

Rym "And make sure you don't let go of the rope when you wash it out!"

Off she went in disgust, shaking her head.

And so, went the travels until after they had passed Florio Island and out in 'Bluewater' over the night the wind and swell had increased measurably. This was something very new and terrifying to some of them.

The swell size was easily three times greater than the ship. It's the first thing you see as you're hanging on to anything, taking the first step out of the companionway, on to the deck. Moving liquid mountains with their tops whipped white from heavy gusts of wind driven rain. Qwe, Oz and Artemis didn't seem to be too bothered,

Rym more concerned about the ladies. Max was talking with the captain and quickly made his way across the heaving deck, making it look easy.

Max "A little blow, captain, thinks by later tonight it will be behind us."

Tamra, with a little scare in her voice, "Are we going to die?"

"Na, you will get used to it."

Still, it's an unnerving experiencing being drawn down into the black troth, along with the anxiety it promotes. Then a few moments later your whole world is looking up at the wave face and wondering when or if you will make the top with wind chop that makes the Sea look like it's steaming.

Presently ascending the face making the very foam filled choppy crest, with a feeling like now you can see the world!

Everything is ok! (For a few seconds). Then you're heading down the backside, and everything happens again and again and ....

Later that evening the wind and rain were such that it was uncomfortable on deck, so they endured the only way they comfortably could, in their cabin hammocks.

Later that evening things did neutralize a lot, everyone came up on deck to stretch their legs very thankfully, the wind was with them, the captain let them know they were making good time and should arrive a day early.

Things fell into the sameness over the next few days, coming up on the starboard side, The Island of Utica. That landmark meant they would be in Palermo tomorrow morning, that was very welcome news, they had made the trip in less than five days.

Making their way off the ship, thanking the captain, Rym asked if he would be available in two weeks.

He informed Rym it would take that long to unload the cargo then reload. Thanking him again Rym joined the group on shore, with a very thankful Mera who had suffered only a minor amount of sickness of the sea.

Tayas & Tamra were also finding themselves to be very pleased with the solid ground rather than the liquid kind.

Still, at times, everybody was hit with small bouts of 'gravity storms,' a curious overhanging feeling of sailing, quickly needing to hang on to something, a short time leftover element of sea travel due to the inner ear.

Max was quickly off with some other shipmates, making inquiries of an unknown nature.

Chapter Thirty-one

Qwe & Tayas were admiring their new surrounds with particular interest to the moderate and some abrupt sloping outskirts of Palermo. They each fostered a thought, 'wonder if she is somewhere up there' concern of a father and mother.

Max surprisingly rejoined the group after a short time, and a question came first from Tamra; when at the Inn they would be staying at, did they have warm bathes? If not, find another place!

All he said was 'follow me' moving away from the waterfront. With what little they carried on their backs through alleys to larger streets, different little marketplaces along the way that Tamra 'just had to look at.' A little hill hiking up city streets had them arriving at piazza Boras Inn.

The owner and Max were friends, shipmates from the past, so the company was offered the nicest view rooms they had.

Also, set-in motion laundry and bathing for any and all with no exceptions. Telling the group, they would rest a day here while he would find his people with any suitable good information also, that he was staying with another group tonight that had a similar goal.

It was with one persisting thought they wished to get the ship grunge off themselves. Inquiries were made before Max left for new clothes that were more like what locals were wearing here presently.

So, before the bath, the daughter of the owner walked them back down to the market area and fitted them all appropriately.

After the freshen-up and all the folderol, they were comfortably assembled in the common room with small lunch items; dried fish and bread and of course, the beverage of the land. Breathing a comforting breath on a static surface, filling the small void with a welcome lunch that was just right.

Now being able to assay the surroundings with more of a coherent understanding of what they were facing,

Qwe "We are relying on Max much too heavily, I am concerned he doesn't move himself away from our original intentions, I don't want to be used for another one of his other purposes."

Rym, "I have an eye on his agenda as well, also I would like to listen carefully tonight after dinner to any talk around the hearth, it seems there is more French spoken here than Latin. Tamra if you would sit with Oz in a different part of the room, Tayas & Qwe the same you will. We need alternant information or something we can compare too"

Oz, "Why don't we just follow him tonight to see where he goes. Artemis and I have our locaters, I can home-in on Tamra if we get lost."

Qwe looking very hesitant" I don't know…"
Tamra slightly waving her hand in the air,

"Don't worry, I told you, they think they're like James Bond, they'll find out what's going on right Oz…Art?"

"Yep, we are not very obvious, the shadows are our friends."

Artemis "I think I like this idea, it's time we had some fun."

Tamra "You know, they even have silencers on the guns they brought just like J. B."

Rym, "We are in a small state of desperation with time and being off-worlders here with no real friends. Only if you are comfortable with your idea…"

Oz "It's just like hunting, nothing to it."
Art "We are actually pretty dam good at it."

Later Max had joined them for dinner and gave some account of his afternoon which was hopeful, saying he had heard some general news about Fidalac and the 'Sicilian vespers war.'

Along with the Romans who were over taxing the Sicilians, it seemed there was much unrest on different fronts.

After his report he mentioned other people to see tonight, and he would be with them tomorrow, so he bid them good night.

Our two guys were outside already mingling with a small group, and easily started following Max in staggered patterns. He wasn't in a hurry, greeting people along the way not stopping long with each, then moving on. Casually making a turn at a very degraded dark alley and disappeared.

Oz carefully, slowly strolled into the same, Artemis soon followed. Their eyes already accustomed to the dim light, but the smells would change from alley to alley. They were easily following another ally that opened up to a street that had numerous 'bars.'

Located off the Main Street, mostly for the enjoyment of sailors and the like, was well populated and made things easy for Oz and Art. Edging out of the ally and along the buildings he had seen Max take another ally that ended at a set of stairs. Oz instead went around the opposite side to look for another way up.

They found the back-yard neighbor to the rear of the two-story house Max was in, had a lattice drying rack for fish.

The night was warm and full of life from the crowds on the streets, so noise was of no concern. Oz found his way up and on to the drying rack, edging over to an open window which he carefully listened in to. Artemis stayed on the ground so he could keep watch. Oz, listening in heard a lot of talk about things that were of no interest for a while then,

Max "This group I am with, they only want a girl, they don't want any money, they don't care about the others the husband and wife. But that may bring a problem at the time of collecting the reward if one is missing, we may not get any!"

Another voice "Max this is too simple, with the business done here, we all sail safely back to Rome. With smiling faces we either steel the girl or kill your friends."

"But the women are all so beautiful, I would hate to kill them."

Very drunk voice "Then we kill the men and sell the women, easy, yes? Ha ah."

Max, "Yah that will do. You do know where the three Romans are hidden, is that right?"

Voice "You have been there before when we were sailors. We supplied a Villa up at 'Sanitaria id Santa Rosalia' (For the reader; This is what the area is called today, at the time our company was there, they had other names that are associated with a spring) you must remember the Villa there."

Max "Ya I do remember that place, it was very large".

"That will make it easier to get in and out of, lots of places to hide."

Other voices "Maybe we should take the women now."

Voice "You think with your ass! First, they are going to pay Max for helping, then we do our business right before we get back to Rome."

With that, they went on about another thing that was of no interest to Oz. Carefully retracing their steps, they soon were back. Getting everybody together they exchanged stories of what the other has learned. Without a doubt Oz's information was of the most interest.

Tamra, "Told you guys, you should check him out with his holder thing on, I'll bet he even has his silencer thing on."

Oz, "That's shoulder-holster, and yes, it is on."

Tamra, "Suppose you two want a martini 'Shaken not stirred' now don't ya." smiling very proud of the two.

"That does sound great, but we will settle for a cup or two of home-grown wine."

Tamra "Deal."

Tayas, sitting back in the common room,

"You don't seem very worried about the possibility of being sold as slaves."

Tamra, "With those two guys on our side, I am not at all worried. You should see him at the moving target range, he took me there once, it was kinda fun."

Oz & Art's information was a true eye opener for all. All agreed to treat Max the same as they have in the past, but with a lot more caution.

At breakfast Max pointed out where they thought she was, up on one of the larger plateaus overlooking the town.

He wanted them to know his group was going up to get a feel for the guards and they might stay overnight. Don't worry if you don't see me till the next day, then he left.

Oz, Artemis, Qwe, Rym, Mera, Tayas and Tamra were all a little puzzled and had the feeling they were getting left behind.

Watching Max leave with his group in a wagon carrying 8 men, Oz was reading everybody mind.

"We passed a stable last night, I could get a driver and a wagon… with straw Tamra… and be back here while everybody packs, Art, grab all our stuff & extra ammo!"

Rym, "Let's go everybody, I think you are on to it."

Oz had little trouble getting both, wagon and a driver the son of the owner who spoke French told him the hay costs extra.

Without asking, Oz was digging into his pocket, came up with what was needed.

At the Inn everybody was loading things, the boy said it would be a good idea to bring lunch things, so the girls asked the lady of the Inn for lunch for the group, and so it was done.

Oz, sitting with the young driver was asking about the road, the boy told him it was cobbled most of the way, and the place was a Holy place. Some new people have taken it over he didn't know anything about them, but they were not good people. Oz asked what he meant by that, the boy just said that all the people that bring them goods to live on are not paid well or treated kindly.

Boy "We can go to the spring but no farther, I don't want them to yell at us"

Oz, "How much farther is it?"

"Oh, not far, just around the next corner up there."
Pointing up over a small ridge,

"There is a nice spot by a little stream before the spring, about 20min away, I'll stop there to rest the horses if that's ok?"

Oz "That sounds just right."

Moving back in the cart to talk with everybody, he told of the spring and the castle a little farther on and making plans for Qwe, Art and himself to go and reconnoiter and of course, being careful not to see Max's group. Stopping at the little stream Oz, could see signs of heavy footprints fresh in the mud.

Lunch was had, Rym was explaining to the boy they didn't want to see anybody else and was asking if the road continued on after the Villa.

The boy was very interested and seemed to be a little intrigued, even started talking softer which gave everybody a quiet smile.

Boy "It winds little then starts to go down to some fishing villages."

Reaching the Spring Qwe & Oz slipped off while Rym helped the boy water the horses and hide the cart.

Chapter Thirty-two

It was a kind afternoon, a small wind flowing through the trees that was natural for the elevation, giving off a whispering comforting sound. Sky was mild, the forest was very thick and was easy to make their way under its cover, almost to the Villa. Strange enough they found the cart Max and his group were using, their horse still tacked together slowly gnawing on the short grass, with no guard, and to close to the front gate.

Art had his eyes on the ground and told Qwe it had the look of a struggle.

Without saying much, it was decided to move away carefully. Once away, things appeared very clearly, horses unattended, the cart being so close to the front gate was evidence enough the men of the villa had taken them.

Back at the spring a new plan came into being. Qwe, Rym, Art and Oz were discussing plans to spend the night to observe the goings on in the Villa and gain entrance. The boy was listening with much interest and excitedly interjected,

"Don't do that, come back down with me now and you can go in on a supply cart."

Everybody was looking at the boy questionably. Rym, "Exactly what are you saying?"

"My father sends a lot of different food and drink things once a week, and two others a husband & wife to help sort things, I usually drive the cart, nobody likes them here."

Oz was way ahead and already volunteered himself, & Tamra,

"It should be us; we can easily start looking around. Tamra can listen to the kitchen people for any news while she helps put things away, and if we run into trouble, she can start a fire for distraction."

The sound of this new plan was something that had merit and could safely be done, so back in the cart and bouncing back down the cobbled road to the Inn. The boy told the company that the supply cart was not going up until Friday and today was Wednesday.

"Friday I will be here early, I will tell my father that I am helping some friends that need work, so he won't ask why I am not taking anybody."

Rym "We will give you extra coins for all your help, but please, don't tell anybody of our plan."

Boy "This is very exciting; I won't tell anyone!"

So, having a day to rest and think of any contingencies, Oz was again cleaning/reloading, Artemis checked on the boy, all was ready to go for tomorrow morning. For the newly found Mom & Dad, the added concern of their child was also tugging at them.

Leaving all that for now, the evening of their rest day found Tayas & Qwe walking hand in hand along the waterfront on a warm starry night.

The two enjoying the aromas of the sea, the open-air restaurants and each other's company. All the Harbor lantern flames shimmering across the mediterranean sea, painted a comfortable feeling of hope to come.

Oz & Art were up earlier getting all of their 'tools' ready to go, with Tamra languishing in bed,

"Hay come on Tamra, get up! Let's go find your sister." That did seem to motivate her a bit more. Artemis was waiting outside for the boy and ready for the hunt.

Quietly seeing them off, Qwe reminded the group he would see them in two days.

This time, Tamra sat with the boy driving their cart. She needing to ask about the kitchen area, also needed to know about the ladies in the kitchen. What about the guards, anything she could think of that might help Oz and herself. The young boy was very helpful, and did mention among other incidentals, sometimes they spent the night in the barn if they were late in getting there.

That gave her a couple of ideas, so she jumped in back with Oz and together another plan was developed. Oz went up to sit with the boy and told him if they could stop at the little stream as Tamra wasn't feeling well.

With that done, she managed to counterfeit being ill most the morning till afternoon, they then continued on to the Villa. The boy seemed to be a little nervous, Oz was sitting next to him asked why.

"When I get there late, they always are mean; I don't like them"

Arriving at the front gate a guard hailed them, the boy answered, and the gate was opened. One of the guards approached,

"Your late! Get over to the kitchen, quick!"

The boy knew where to place the cart, jumping down on scattered hay, he walked over to a large wooden door banging with his fist, they didn't have long to wait.

"What's this, so late! You just missed a beating, bring in the stuffs, hurry now!"

Trip after trip loading vegetables in one room meats in a cold room down some stairs. On one of the trips, Oz and Art stepped off a little to investigate and found only hallways and rooms. Nothing really here, so back on up to find Tamra putting more things away on shelves. So, it went for some time.

The kitchen ladies sent them in a different direction, the boy and Oz took a number of trips upstairs to a serving-staging area. There Oz looked in on what was the main serving hall, not really big, but very elegant. Not wanting to pause to long, headed back down with the boy. At this point they were told to drive the cart to the guest house kitchen and unload what they have left and to take the girl to help the servant there.

Tamra was talking with Oz

"I forgot to ask Mera how I identify my sister, what am I supposed to look for?"

Oz "That again is another good question, but I have no idea."

At the back door of the guest Villa a lot smaller, but still very nice. The boy knocking, the lady greeting him was better sounding but still needed the things off the cart quickly. As the unloading of the same things but in lesser quantities.

Tamra was told to take the wine to dining room, never having been there, only guessing by the turn of the lady's chin, she turned down a long hallway, then into a large room that was clearly a living room, noticing three people reading or lounging by a fire.

Unconsciously pausing over long, she found herself staring…. At herself!

The gentleman vaguely noticed her pause and said "Tizz' about time, thank you yes, we would like to refill our cups."

Tamra could hardly respond,

"I, I am not the server" as politely as was possible for her. The man "Nonsense, you are here, be so kind."

Holding out his cup… so she obliged,

"Yes, of course…"

Setting down one of the decanters she made her way around the room, carefully filled each cup until she came to the last. Trying not to glance, but of course she did anyway, found the girl looking at her rather closely.

Tamra knew it was 'Lyka' her sister! And yes, she could see a very unique look to her aura. What she really wanted to say and do was,

'How the hell are ya? And give me a hug, I'm your sister!'

Something like that. Congratulating herself on the fact of not spilling anything, she turned and placed the decanter on the table.

On her departure with the smallest glance back, she noticed the girl looking still after her, but not making a note of it to her people.

Tamra on the other hand lost it! She was talking to herself in English walking down the hallway to the kitchen. Finding Oz, grabbing his sleeve pulled him outside, (still in English)

"Oz it her, it's her, she's her, is here!"

Oz holding her shoulders asked her to explain

"How did you know "

Tamra "She, she looked at me!"

Oz "Ah, we are going to need a little more than that!"

"No, she looked at me and I looked at her!"

"Tamra, please calm, let's try that again"

"Ok, ok… wait!! She looks just like me!!!"

Oz "Wow! Really! That simple?"

Tamra "She looked at me the whole time I was there."

Oz "All right we gotta finish this stuff, they told us we can stay in the stable tonight."

"I, I, gotta call mom! Oh yea, no phone. I can't wait to tell mom!"

As they were heading to the stable, Art was asking Oz privately about Tamra,

"What's the deal with her, she ok? "

Oz "We found what we are looking for follow me."

Art "Way cool! Let's go figure something!"

The two disappeared trying to survey more of the property, locate other rooms and taking note of windows along the way. They're heading back towards the stables when the lady from the main kitchen bumped into them and let them know to take some things for dinner. They thanked her and went back to the kitchen, while they filled their wooden plates, she told Artemis to take the slop to the prisoners.

"I am sorry ma' lady I don't know where that is."

Kitchen Lady "Haven't you been here before? You look like one that has, well, this one will take ya."

She was pointing at the boy, so off they went down a few steps. Then along a short torch lamplit hall to a left turn and a bank of thick wooden doors with slots at eye level and one on the bottom.

Art looked through the first and did recognize Max but made no call to him.

Sliding the plates under the door, walked away without a word. Noticing the heavy sliding piece of wood for a door-latch, he would think on that and let Oz know.

Out in the stable, getting themselves settled as they could, good fresh hay and a heavy horse blanket for each. Art, Oz & Tamra were speaking in English and trying to come up with what to do with everybody, for now Oz had the best answer he thought.

"Since all the guards were posted along the parameter wall, none seemed to be roaming the grounds yet. I'll locate sister, then drop her here. Tamra could make something move around, distract the kitchen help, then Art could move to let out Max and his group. Then you start a big fire in the kitchen, those other guys are on their own, we have our cart ready and away we go. On the way out of here, we…. you, start the main gate on fire! Easy!"
Tamra, "Your nuts, what if the guards come after us?"

Oz "Simple…we shoot 'em."
Art "Remember, these are the bad guys."

Tamra "Don't you think we need more help?"

Oz "No, it would mean more people to get down the hill and that would hold us up!"

Tamra "What about the boy?"

Oz "I think that kid is going to love it! I'll tell the boy enough but not too much, this all hasta happen late tonight so try to rest a little."

After giving the boy just enough information, he seemed to be very keenly interested in the whole idea, and wanted to know what language he and Tamra were speaking in,

Oz "It's called English"
Just for fun he added,

"It hasn't been thought of yet."
The boy held a lasting, very confused look on his face.

Chapter Thirty-three

About 12:30 they commenced their mission with a new moon and thin ribbons of altostratus clouds overhead. Art had been timing the guards, with an old fashion wind up watch that wasn't even invented yet.

Oz & Art knowing what to expect, quietly headed to the little Villa. Sticking to shadows, listened for clanking swords, footsteps, random talk, anything. Art, using hand signals indicated he was going around the far side.

Oz, coming up to a very steep drop off on one side of the Villa, slowly edged along under some windows.

Noticing flickering candlelight, found the small dining room with the view he had seen earlier.

Very carefully he knelt by an open window and listened in, it seemed they too were in talks of escape they spoke in Greek, knowing the slaves could not understand.

That presented Oz with another hurtle as well, he only was just passable with his understanding of it. But understanding enough, he moved closer to the parameter wall crawling on hands and knees came around corner in the dark and,

"Who are you! Stand up!"

Oz stayed calm, as he stood up, he reached under his jacket and turning around easily and drawing his pistol quietly took care of the guard without another sound.

He then drug the guard over to the canyon and shoved him off the cliff. Another 'pruff, pruff' put him quickly on alert. Slowly moving around another corner, he found Artemis dragging another body over to the canyon edge and pushing it off.

Getting back under the cover of the building and shadows, they looked up and noticed two more guards on the wall parapet moving closer to investigate, it seemed to Oz, the guard was just about ready to sound an alarm. Art, again neatly wiped out his 9mm and "pomf."

The momentum threw one of the guards off the wall and into the canyon. Oz at the same time had done the same thing with another look-out, they knew that things had to start happing fast, in case the guards were checking in with each other at a cretan time.

So not seeing any other guards on this side of the Villa, Oz asked Art with a whisper

"Hey, your Greek is better than mine, go in, tell them to wait for a commotion over at the other villa, then come out here. You or I will meet them here"

Art entered a side door, quietly moving along a short hallway, following the flickering light and found the dining room. Hiding in the shadows he tried whispering his best Greek, getting their attention with a finger over his mouth,

Art "Shish, I am help."

He whispered in French,

"I am here to help you get out! if you understand drink wine"

Calmly lifting their cups, remaining silent,

"Is anybody watching?"

The man announced in a quiet voice as if talking to his wife,

"Not really"

Art decided to sneak to the far side of the table with the most cover of the back wall and slip under.

A few moments later, in came a servant with wine, serving each one then leaving. Art crawled over to the man and whispered the plan,

"Just wait for the fire in the big kitchen, then go to this far side of the villa, stay in the shadows, I will come back."

Art had come up with an addition to the escape plan. The man said he was a military man and asked for a sword, Art suggested a knife from the table, it was all he could do for now.

Moving back outside, carefully thinking of what was left of the guards, started for the stables to meet up with Oz. Sliding around a corner, he came face to face with another guard patrolling the grounds. Before the guard could speak, he quick stepped back, while easily pulling the gun and "pomf, pomf."

The problem was the cliff was a way off, so dragging the guard behind a water trough close by would have to do.

Quietly entering the stable, he noted the horses rigid and wagon ready, Tamra and Oz seemed right on target, nodding to the boy,

Oz "We will be back soon."

Out the three went from the front of the stable making some noise with their wine cups in hand, waved at a guard on the opposite parapet on the way to the kitchen. Taking note on how many there were, then headed into the prep area Oz was looking at Tamra and whispering,

"Ok with the fire fingers?"

"Yep!"

Walking into the kitchen Art asked for more wine, one of the other ladies just pointed then turned back to her work, that gave a little extra time for Tamra to set her sights on a large sack of oats ... next,

"Wapomww"

Oz "My girl! You over did it just right!"

Tamra, absolutely amazed with herself "Wow!"

The few people that were in the area were all of a sudden very animated, running around looking for buckets and water! Art knew the way to the holding room, Oz and Tamra followed on, running down the touch lit hall, turning left, Oz pointed to an unlit torch, and she did it again, lighting the torch on the run.

Art was opening the cell door, Max and his group were already on their feet, hearing all the disturbance and couldn't understand it. Starting to ask questions, Oz just told him his cart was still outside the gate, you are on your own, talk later…with that, they ran out as Tamra left a wake of small fires everywhere!

Everybody was in a panic in the kitchen, what was left of the courtyard guards were starting to get buckets of water bring them down the hall. As they ran past Tamra for some reason, they would drop or trip on something and spill their water.

Then arguments broke out and fighting amongst themselves, Art was thinking this is the perfect get a way scene. Now Art, & Oz moved with Tamra to the small villa and around the far side, panic, yelling and confusion was a little behind them.

They did find the waiting captives right where they planned,

Art "Follow us, there's a wagon in the stable!"

Oz, on the run, asked Tamra if she would start another fire out here, while the others were thinking about the kitchen.

The guards were fully involved with the fires in both locations. Oz reaching the stable, found the boy was more than ready, he had already opened the front gate with Maxes help.

With everybody in the wagon, they were out and away much faster than even they thought! Oz got Tamra's attention and pointed "Could you…?"

Even before he finished both sides of the gate were engulfed in flame. There was a guard on the wall yelling his head off, Oz taped Artemis, they both wanted him quiet, so very casually they both took out their 9mm's and "pummf..pummf"

That help restored a reasonable sense of peace to the place. Tamra looked at Oz's face "You're smiling?"

Oz, "It was a long shot! Not really easy to protect the girl I love."

Tamra "Aww"

Artemis smiled, nobody else knew what was going on.

The boy was driving fast but being careful, the weather was really starting to turn stormy. Oz asked him to pull over at the stream down the hill farther, with a determined look, the boy felt he had saved the whole day! Everybody of course, gave him high marks.

When the trothing and bouncing hay cart slowed, Tamra and the girl were still staring at each other. As the cart stopped Oz helped each one out and started to introduce everybody,

Tamra stepped up first,

"Hi, my name is Tamra, yours is Lyka and I am your sister!"

Everybody looked at everybody, Art, Oz & Tamra were the only ones laughing, Tamra hugging Lyka her sister for the first time, stepped back and easily said,

"You won't believe it, even when we can explain it!"

The husband and wife still with questions had grateful expressions on.

Oz "No time now, put your coats on and hoods up, we gotta get away from here!"

And so, our boy hero drove them safely back with a very confident air. Art asked if the boy could take them to the back of the Inn and not say a word to anybody! He would find him tomorrow.

Oz took them straight up the back stairs and into their rooms. Everybody was more than likely at dinner, so Tamra and Art stayed with the three, Oz went down to locate the others.

Finding everyone very excited, it seems Max had already been by telling everything but in little detail. Tayas couldn't wait! She ran upstairs and at the door, walking right in and with one short glance, she knew she was hugging her daughter Lyka.

Chapter Thirty-four

Ok, hold it. Who are these new people you ask? Well, the new people were asking themselves the same question, how do you know I am your sister! And thanks for the rescue, but who are all of you. Let's start with the new folks to Tamra.

The husband and wife were members of the Roman senate, they were kidnaped because they were thought to have magic. The same was true for Lyka since she was originally from Scotland, and a Princess.

When they arrived here, the man Fidalac made them show him their skills, when he found out in-fact they had none, he set a higher ransom on them.

As far as the husband & wife, nice people an all, but we don't care about them right now, later maybe.

Lyka on the other hand, was right up front with questions giving Tamra a good run for her money.

Before all the talk between mom and her two daughters got into detailed past and deeper future plans, Rym thought it wise to invite the husband & wife downstairs for some dinner. First offering them some dry clothes, they declined, then escorting them downstairs.

In the meantime, Tayas started asking questions of Lyka. How much did she know about magic, also what she knew about her captor?

Lyka... First off, she wanted to know who we were and how she looked so much like Tamra.

Tamra "You are not going to get it at first"

Lyka "Get what?"

Tamra mildly frustrated, worded it differently,

"Ok, you aren't going to believe me when I tell you that this is your mother, and this is your father and guess what? I am your sister!"

Lyka didn't let things get by her easily,

"All right but how is all this possible, my supposed mom and dad setting right here, look the same age as I am!"

Tamra "Don't worry about all that stuff right now, details are for later it will take too long to explain, just stick with me for now and listen... Wait a sec. mom are we twins?"

Tayas stopping for a moment,

"I have no idea! Nice question"

Lyka turned to Tayas and asked

"Why does Tamra talk so different?"

Tamra "Hay mom I got this one, it's because we are from a different future time, kinda cool hu!"

Lyka was starting to think she had fallen in with a bunch of lunatics, and Tayas kinda had a feeling she was feeling that way, so

"Lyka, watch me."

Tayas pointed with two fingers and extinguished the candles then....

Tamra breaking in,

" Lem-me! Lem-me!"

And Tamra actually did a neat job of relighting the candles!

Lyka, was all of a sudden trying to add all this up, to put some things in perspective, slowly. Realizing she must be very tired and Tayas took note of her rumblings of hunger, and decided to change the direction of the evening, asking if she would like dinner downstairs. With a change of clothes and added smudges on her face, down they all went.

Chapter Thirty-five

Rym had a nice table by the fire, with the weather not being good at all, the common room was all most full. Getting Lyka settled with snacks and wine, she began recovering quickly. She needed a warm fire, and some small talk, it was previously decided not to talk openly, thinking to herself what a day!

With no one really noticing, a huge man entered soaking wet, came over and sat right on the hearth in front of the group. Nobody bothered the man with a long white beard, cold and wet from outside, letting him warm up.

Qwe volunteered "Rough night to be abroad…"

"I haven't come far, but we must get back."

As the man was talking Mera was looking at him very closely, then got up and leaned in to whisper,

"Ambrosius, how in the world?"

"Yes, Mera, you have found me out… I am here to tell you the captain you all came with will mean you harm soon. Everybody except the man and woman must get ready for a small trip, a few km. to a cave. Get your things quietly now."

Around the Company she went telling everyone their next move, and up they went. Merlin started talking to the other two telling them to,

"Be very careful, Max will want to return you to Rome, be on your guard when you get to Rome."

They wanted to know how they were going to pay, and who he was.

Merlin "That all is done."

That was all he said, standing, he waited by the door leaning on his staff, (for the reader, when have you ever heard of a wizard not owning a staff or a staff owning him. It's their modus operandi of course Merlin has a staff!) He had not long to wait, everyone was prepared for wind, rain and thunder.

Well, you will guess who their driver was, the young boy, chomping at the bits, ready to go, and so they did.

Merlin sat with the boy and told him to go to 'Sorgenti del Gabriele' which wasn't far. With the rain pelting them along with the wind, lightening/thunder, they were happy to eventually get inside. The group wasn't sure what they were in; there was a rough wooden door that opened to a domed cave with a spring in one tunnel. The boy was curious and felt no shame in asking,

"My father told me that magic things happen in this place, are they going to happen again?"

Merlin looked directly, firmly.

"It will"

The boy looking closely at him,

"Yu, you're that, man from Scotland!"

"Yes, now be off, your father will worry."

The Company thanked the boy, also thanked him with handfuls of coins, then turned to the business at hand.

Merlin had everyone gather around as he explained that this was a place that had crystals similar to his cave. That he would slowly walk around the group, stay close together, it might take some time, they must wait for lightning close by.

Slowly he started humming some incantation and he kept going, twenty minutes or more, as he was holding his staff high with a crystal in his other hand,

kirrrkkboom!

They started… Tamra was holding Lyka's hands she was very unsure, then already fading back in, they were standing in a very familiar spot,

Tayas "Alva glen, I love Alva glen! Oh, I am so glad!"

Mera "Merlin! I could kiss you! I don't have a long boat trip in front of me!"

Oz, "Hold up, there is somebody in our cave!"

Art was already on the defensive

Merlin, "My helper had made that fire before I left, let's get out of this storm here."

Everybody piled into the second cave, there were blankets and food to be made and wine. Lyka was very tired and what she first asked was,

"Are we traveling any more tonight? And you are Merlin Ambrosius, a lot older that I thought."

Qwe "She's starting to sound like Tamra already!"

Merlin, "This is a traveling shape, it's uncomfortable to change, so, this is how you see me for now."

As the good smells of the rabbits started to roast and permeate the cave, everybody started getting dried off at the fire...sitting in a circle,

Tayas "Merlin I have a question, were the girl's triplets?"

Merlin "For some reason I don't remember right now, let me think on that."

Tayas, in a sing song voice...

"I think you are toying with me!"

Clearing his voice,

"Now my hearing is not so good"

Tayas turned "And I didn't think he had a sense of humor..."

Smiling at Mera, small laughs.

The next morning Tamra was all over Lyka with questions,

"So, do you want to move things around with your finger or start a fire? Well, what do you think?"

Lyka was really starting to wonder when all this new information coming in was going to sort of slow down,

"Tamra, I am new at all this, so be slow with me, ok?"

Tayas overheard Tamra,

"You can't go in without me, and it's still raining and too cold right now, this afternoon maybe."

Tamra "Au, mom it's all warm when the 'Lake lady' is there."

"No" …

Breakfast was oat cakes, beef jerky, tea, Merlin had Rym, Qwe and Oz siting by the morning fire looking at the Collider calendar with Mera, in two days there would be another test. Those days would be needed for Rym to talk to Merlin about the future events, also to decide where Lyka would be best suited.

With the storm passing, there was a measure of rain, not much but enough to keep them in the cave.

After hours of talk and questions, mostly from Lyka, Tamra wanted to show Oz, Art and Lyka the crystal caves. Grabbing Qwe's light Tayas handed it to Tamra,

"No thanks, that's no fun, I have my own"
She held up a torch.

Tayas, "Don't burn the cave down!"

Off they went, Mera wanted to ask what they thought about Lyka staying here or going back with them to Meyrin. It went back and forth a little, but Tayas put her foot down and finally decided that she should go back to stay with her, the rest would be decided later. The balance of the day was lazy for all.

The next morning was just right, almost no clouds above, no wind it was a hiking day for some. For others it was study, Mera and Merlin were going over the rune book, Rym, Qwe were writing notes, they only brought one small book of paper, so they tore it in half and shared the single pencil.

A reasonably warm afternoon gave Tamra the idea for another shot at jumping in, Tayas was agreeable. Oz & Art were not invited, so back to the cave for the men.

Tayas said she would be first, then the two could jump in. Splash! 'The lady of the lake' welcomed her,

"Your highness has someone else to introduce?"

"I do and I'll be right back"

Popping up, all she said was "Come on girls!"

Double splash!

"Tayas, would you do the honor"

"Yes, but I think she needs to breath"

Up and down, Lyka, slowing her thought,

"Yes… I am here"

'Lady of the lake' this is my daughter Lyka"

" It is a wonderful honor to meet you Princess Lyka."
Up and down once more,

"Welcome princess Tamra"

"Thank you, ma,' lake lady"

Tamra "Hay Lyka, we forgot to tell you, you're a real princess! sorry everyone,"

Nyneve "Tayas your family is growing again I am aware Lyka has many thoughts, all will be answered in time."

Tayas "Rym and Mera have traveled to the future looking for Carisa, we know little now, but we will keep going."

"Have much caution there, for now I will give you calm, and we will all see each other soon, I must be off."

Tayas "Thank you Ma 'lady"

The water was warm now so slowly getting out, Lyka was again feeling so much change in so little time, asking Tayas,

"Am I to anticipate these new things happening every day?"

Tayas "I know all this is very overwhelming at first, and no, your introduction has finished, for a time."

Tamra "That felt great, how does it feel to be a princess, oops, I remember you already were one, whatever. Can you pick-up your shoes over there?"

Lyka, pointed with two fingers and accidentally spread her fingers and all of a sudden, her sandals burst into flames!

Tamra fell back in the warm water laughing so hard. Tayas immediately had the fire under control, and did laugh a little herself…

Tayas, "Only with one and think of what you want to move."

Lyka pointing with one finger, with determination on her face…over floated the smoldering sandals!

Lyka "Hay, I am a fairy for real! Wow."

Tamra, "Hay you sound like me 'Wow.' I say it all the time, I don't know why. Hay you fairy, how come your sandals are crispy?"

Lyka "You really want to know? I'll show you!"

At that moment Lyka turned, ran back in the water and tackled a surprised Tamra on the way! The bubbling two came up laughing and hugging.

Tayas was looking at the two girls now clean for the first time and realized she was looking at a mirror, size, color hair.,. Thinking it was starting to feel as it should be, almost...

Tamra had an idea as they were walking back to the cave,

"Lyka, just for fun, walk-in and sit next to Oz, just want to see if he can tell any difference."

Lyka was unfamiliar with Tamra's sense humor, so she thought twice, but what the heck.

Oz was idly writing something, Lyka sat down next to him, and he leaned over and started to give Tamra (he thought) a quick kiss, then

"Aa, I, I, woo sorry! I thought...."
Looking at them both with clean faces and Oz pointing,
"She put you up to this! (Giving Tamra a sour look) Sorry Lyka, Tamra you're trying to get me in trouble!"

Everybody laughing Tamra, had to ask how Oz was able to tell who was who,

Tamra "How could you know?"

Oz, quickly thinking he could get back at her a little...

"It is easy, Lyka's hair is always neat."

The evening was pleasant, Merlin had a few ideas or possible leads for their search. Over a campfire dinner, Rym was in deep conversation with Merlin, and wanted to know if he had an interest in coming back with them to Meyrin (Switzerland)

"No, I have been to your future times, and I care not for them."

Mera was in a quandary about how he knew we needed help when everybody was in Sicily,

Merlin "Hum. I knew this question would arise, so, I may guess you know of the 'Lady' and myself,"

Tayas, "I do remember a little history on the subject

Tamra "You have the hots for her!"

Tayas "Tamra! Please show some respect!"

Tamra "Sorry your Merliness."

Small laughs around, even Merlin found it amusing.

"Yes, since that is what is in your history books, I won't dispute that now. She, as you know, can have a presents in fresh water almost anywhere. She saw you depart Rome and found you in Sicily. She has her ways that I know not of. I have many crystals and have traveled far, the one I gave you I borrowed form that man Anthony, he is most responsible for this trouble. I changed shape and learned much of his dealings while working with him years ago. This is why I thought that crystal has significance."

Qwe, "Are we to confront him if we see him again?"

Merlin, "No, do not put yourself in danger in that way, he has many ways to defend himself."

That put Oz to thinking of different ways to defend their self's in the future. Art was thinking the same thing.

Breakfast the next day was more of a pack up and get ready, the test time was earlier than usual. Bidding Merlin adieu, this time everybody joined hands and phased back to Meyrin, Switzerland.

Lyka was again overwhelmed, and Tayas could tell,

"Lyka, I forgot about this part when I said your introduction was done, well…now it's done. For a while…again…"

A 12 Th. century girl in a physics lab in Switzerland, she remained silent. Dr. J was as usual overjoyed, and taking in the similarities with a quick note, asking,

Dr. J "I trust all is well, and we have a newcomer I see"

Rym, "Don't forget, Latin, Dr. Not English"

"Welcome, I am Dr. Johnstone"

"I, I am Lyka."

Reluctantly very unsure of her surroundings, sitting down,

Tayas "Tamra would you take Lyka to the guest room showers and give her some new clothes, oh be sure to show her how the shower works!"

Tamra taking Lyka by the hand, "You are going to love the shower, come on!"

Dr. J was telling them he was very thankful they arrived when they did. In one week, they were shutting down the Collider for three weeks, maintenance issues. All were very happy about that; it will give everybody time to collect themselves. The men said they we're off to shower and change on their side of the gym and would be back soon. Tayas & Mera did the same with the girls.

As they were discussing the trip, Oz had already talked with Artemis, Qwe and Rym, he didn't want to tell the women about taking all the guards out, and it was understood between them to keep it quiet just for now.

It was without any argument from any of the weary travelers they would all go to 'R-4' (For the reader: It's what they like to do! CERN employees, local fast Italian favorite)

Tayas wanted to explain to Lyka again about new customs, Tamra sat with Lyka explaining the settings, the eatery and music.

During dinner it was decided that Lyka would stay with mom & dad first, Tayas could stay home and be with Lyka for the first week, Tamra had to reappear at work to get caught up. Artemis had to get back to Sterling not only for his other job, but Athena was wanting to know all about the adventure, and she really missed her boy.

Dr. J, Mera, Rym, and Qwe spent many days in reviewing every part of the trip, Mera was making notations on the runes they had gone over, updating all museum library records.

One evening, Tayas invited the group over for dinner, the idea was to discuss who would go on the next trip.

Rym felt they should take another small reconnaissance trip, it was debated a number of ways but, Lyka, Tamra & Tayas were finally decided on for a short trip.

Rym composed a Map, the best he could recall, locating the crystal room, then walking to Emily's apartment. If they couldn't locate Emily or Lisa then to maybe hang out at the kiosk plaza, hopefully find them or they would 'see' them.

Tayas keep forgetting to explain things to Lyka - TVs, cars, refrigerators and canned food. Qwe & Tayas have a cat for a house pet. That was very strange for Lyka but had the hardest time with the moving carts with no horses, and all the things in a bathroom.

After the first week, Tamra couldn't wait to get her hands on Lyka, and take her out to a real restraint/night club.

After dinner while at a night spot Tamra, kindly asked Oz to show Lyka how to dance. Apparently, she liked to dance back in Rome, in her way, which was very different, but she seemed to get right into it. She wouldn't dance with people that asked her, Tamra tried to explain it's not serious, just for fun. Nope, she wasn't going for it.

After they all got back to Tamra's apartment, there were again lots more questions to be answered. Tamra asked Oz how it was to dance with two of her,

"Twice as nice and twice tired, let's to do it all again."

What also really confounded Lyka were cellphones, a little box that talks to other people and she can talk back! She was even starting to watch daytime television! (Oh no!)

Rym and Dr. J were going over how they could make clothes like what Rym & Mera were wearing, decided they couldn't match the fabrics, so hopefully Tayas & Tamra would hook-up with Emily soon after their arrival.

Oz was worried about their safety and had an idea that Tamra should take a Tazer. She was comfortable with handling it, but wanted to bring it up with Qwe, Dr. J and Dr. Rym first.

With the departure time drawing near, Tayas wanted to ask some questions of Mera, about what Emily or Lisa looked like,

"Well, just kinda normal, your age, not anything unusual everybody kinda looks the same. The buildings all float which is kinda different. That little plaza is nice to hang around in.

I couldn't tell you how to get into their apartment all-thou, everything is voice or fingerprint recognition anyway.

So, I do hope they find you or you find them quickly. I wonder if you wore the clothes that I wore back here, then you could see if the machine will let you order clothes for Tamra, then again for yourself."

Tayas "I'll do that, it's worth a shot make it look like we know what we are doing…may-be."

Chapter Thirty-six

Standing at their starting marks with everybody watching. The familiar harmonic vumming started, the two started to phase… then shimmering to nothing.

Lyka standing watching in aw, Qwe was watching her, and had to admit,

"Don't feel left out, we don't know how it works either…yet."

With a smile and a shrug of his shoulders,

"We are still figuring this out. What do you feel about tonight? would you like to stay at Tamra's or at our house?"

Lyka "I'll stay with you dad? Sorry, I'm still getting use to all the changes."

Qwe "That's happening with me also."

They both decided on Italian at R-4, with a lot of small talk for dessert.

Phasing into the crystal room with Tayas & Tamra,

"Wow! This place is different! And there's crystals everywhere. Wonder if I should take one?"

Tayas, "I don't think that would be a wise idea, we don't know where or when it would take you."

Tamra "Ok, you've got a point, they do have tags thou."

Following their map out the hallway, then the large lecture hall, and outside,

It is almost unbelievable for them! Slowly taking everything in, they wandered the plaza looking very touristy, they accidentally stumbled on the kiosk. Tayas asked Tamra to stand on a circle on the floor, as before a scanning device popped from a wall for 20 seconds,

Tayas "Now go behind the screen and take your things off and wait."

Minutes later, down the dispenser came a new change of clothes. Out she came looking just as drab as everybody else, definitely not happy with the look. Tayas was next and had the same results. Well, off to the jacket/coat kiosk! Still wandering in wonder along the way.

Emily at her apartment, had a notice someone was using her acct. at the clothes kiosk, so walking over she easily found them and introduced herself.

"Hello, you two must have had a long-short trip"

Tayas looking closely, and for the first time she 'saw' Emily and bleared out "It's one of us!"

Emily thought that was funny, and laughed

"Welcome! My name is Emily, I see just the two of you once more, is their anyone else?"

Tayas "No, we decided another short trip was in order, how did you know we were here?''

"When the clothes kiosk was in use, one of my icon lights on my coat came on and imagined it must be your group."

"Hi, I'm Tamra and this is …"

Emily "Tayas, mother of the three, with your father's help we were started on a quest, and possibly getting closer to the location of Carisa.

Let's get the two of you some real fashionable over-coats for communications, and then head over to my place."

Rym had shown everybody how his coat worked at the Lab, so noting was really new to them.

Emily ordered bags for their extra clothes, with actual designs on them that were different from all the rest.

It wasn't that far to Emily's apartment, and she wanted to introduce them to the workings there.

They were just starting to get acquainted, Lisa (Emily's partner) had just walked in and was surprised with more guests, she reminded Emily, they now had two different people they must call before they left for dinner.

So, calls were made, and all would be taken care of tomorrow.

Tayas was not all that taken by all the pop-up holograms and pockets, on the other hand, Tamra was stoked! The evening didn't last long because the start of tomorrow would be early.

As the day started, Lisa would meet them at their second stop. Tayas, Tamra and Emily were scheduled to meet Paul the Clairvoyant.

Arriving and being shown in early at Paul's Office, he didn't need introductions, but he did ask some of the same thing as Merlin did.

"May I look at your hand, and also your eyes, each at a time?"

Tayas was first and greeted this man, as did Tamra and as before no comments about the exam. Turning back to their seats he addressed Tamra first,

"You have a strong gift as you have already demonstrated.

You are charged with the greatest single gifts that will bring the circle to a close and the magic contained where it originated. It was never meant to be taken abroad.

You will again meet many difficulties and you should not be left alone. Take the one who helped the most last time, Lyka, Qwe should be amongst your new group. Take no more than that, the information I have received is she might be on one of two Worlds.

These are called Water earths. The land area is limited to 9% But there are large cities under the water that is why I can't clearly see Carisa if she is there. We have the destination crystals you will need."

"The sooner the three are united the sooner the change will begin. It may not happen the first time, be persistent."

Tamra, "Will this be the last trip I go on?"

"No, not at all." was all he said.

Tayas was thinking out loud as they left the meeting,

"I'm not sure I understand what he said about 'not working the first time."

Tamra "Yeah, and what's the deal with everybody wanting to see our hands and eyes? It's creepy…"

At the next stop it turned out to be more of a geography session with charts and maps for all to get familiar with.

Finally, seeing a physical map of where they were presently, Tayas asked about their location which, with the large, protected bay, looked to her like San Francisco, USA of her time.

Emily "Yes, it was called that 800 years ago"

Tayas mentioned not noticing the bridge and were told apparently it was deconstructed and rebuilt in a museum out in the desert next to another smaller bridge.

With the advent of floating transportation, it was deemed unnecessary. They were asked to study their maps of the three worlds, telling them traveling in the Water worlds will have to be quick because of the territory that must be covered.

With the introduction to geography done, and maps all keenly stored in their over-coat memory, they all decided diner on the coast would be fun, different place but the same spectacular overview of the ocean.

After dinner Tamra had to ask if they have night clubs here, both Emily and Lisa said in unison,

"Are you joking?"

Probity shouldn't have done that. They had to drag Tamra out. She was floating with a wine glass in her hand and didn't want to leave! Tayas kinda liked the ideal also but wasn't so defiant as Tamra was about leaving.

On the ride home, Tayas wanted to asked Emily what were some of the quirky natures of the people in Water earths.

Emily "They are a very untrusting collection of people, both Worlds are. Their history is more than not the root of it. Even to this day, the governments change far too often and that is another reason why the magic must be contained. It must be reinstituting back on its source earth. There are no physical wars, just behind the scenes movement of people, mostly with over inflated egos.

Changing the subject, Tamra needed to know something and asked Emily,

"The gifts we all have here in this group are all the same, that is except for my gift, which is greater."

At that she asked, "Why is it that my gifts, I am told are greater, I sure, don't feel any different."

Emily "You must ask Mera, she possesses some of the equivalent gifts, not the same as yours, but I think it's a good place to start. Why do you have more? I have no idea, a good question for 'Paul' next time you get back here."

Next afternoon, they were in the crystal room waiting on the departure time for a while, Tamra, still had a strong feeling about taking a crystal. There were random loose ones scattered all around she didn't know where the desire was coming from. Reaching out her hand to grasp one, it didn't feel right.

Starting to withdraw her hand, then reversed and reaching farther past the first one, comfortably picking up the right feeling one. Tossing it in the bag and a few minutes later they started to phase.

———

Everybody involved was present on the phase-in, with interest in what was found out. Yes, there was lot's to plan for, but the group felt two weeks of greatly needed rest and regrouping was important. Each one of the companies wanted to take things a little slower.

They did find that they all were still thinking about finding Carisa over the two lazy weeks, office life was starting to get a little back to normal and mundane. So, they fell back into more time planning the event coming up. Map & charts were down loaded strategies and member lists were made along

Tamra, Oz, Qwe and Lyka were happily anticipating the trip, and were making ready and in one week they would phase. Dr. J had been wearing one of the jackets for a number of days and figured out how to input all info about the entire effort so far.

Oz found that the jacket accommodated most all the defense items he planned to take along.

Tamra told him he looked fat with all the extra stuff! He reluctantly agreed and put most of his things in a backpack.

On their return from her last trip, Tamra had only mentioned to Mera about the crystal she picked up for some reason and inquired about the degrees of her gifts. According to Mera, she could pick-up large objects, breath under water, physically direct people towards or away from her. That was the extent of what Mera was able to show her, more than that she would have to go seek Merlin out.

Mera felt that Tamra was directed to acquire that one crystal and knowing the circumstances in which they function, she would introduce it as needed accordingly.

Dr. J had developed a gelatin looking crystal that could be sent and received in the phase in phase out without human's present, and at a distance passed as a crystal, the nice part was it acted like a thumb drive with the jackets, hold it on the inside and it would upload or download… keno, Dr. J.

Armed with much, but laden with little, their last information was Dr. J telling them to put the receiving crystal in an out of the way spot.

Soft pleasant vumming started, the focus was blurring looking again, like an old fashion tv had just been turned off. Then back on slowly, finding themselves in the crystal room. Oz placing the communication crystal off a bit on the pile, all headed to the clothes kiosk for Lyka and Oz.

Being informed about Tamra's return with a visual reminder from her coat, Emily headed for the clothes kiosk. Lyka again was really wondering if she was losing her mind, Tamra noticed it and came to her rescue.

"I know this all is overwhelming; it is for me too."
Emily found familiar faces at the kiosk.

"Hello Tamra, how was your trip?"

"Oh, hi Emily! Just great, how are you two?"

"We haven't changed, you've brought a bigger group, now who have we?"

"This is my dad Qwe, and my sister Lyka, oh, and my boyfriend Oz."

"My name is Emily, and I am glad you are all here"

Qwe "We certainly are grateful for greeting us, I will only ask that Lyka will need a time to acclimate she is from the 12th century and only speaks Latin or French"

Emily "I can set the translator on her coat to which ever she prefers, it looks as if you are all most dressed, lets step over to the coat kiosk and get fitted."

Tamra again tried to explain the machine to Lyka, as she was trying to foster the new sensations of this world. Out she came with a translating coat, then off to Carisa's apartment. Along the walkway, the new group was staring at everything in amazement, putting new questions in mind for later.

At the apartment Emily was giving them a brief look at the fowling day's appointments, 'Paul' was at the top of the list. Also, another run out to the coast for some geography introduction. Everyone enjoyed the evening, Qwe specially liked spending time with Lyka, shall we say, a tamer version of Tamra.

So then, an old fashion continental breakfast was had, then the first next stop, 'Paul.'

Once again, he asked to look at Lyka's hands and eyes, once again, didn't explain why. No real conformation of new locations of where 'Carisa' might be found.

Then off to some instruction facility for a quick instruction on the use of the vehicles the Water worlds use. While there, also in the event they did have to be in the water, a small breathing/goggle device that fit in their pocket.

Tamra with the usual self-confident flair,

"I don't need that stuff; I can breathe underwater."

The only respect she got was a 'Wow' from Lyka, everyone else just glared at her with small smiles, capricious punk! With that taken care of, they wanted to head for the coast again, the sun set was calling, Emily wanted to take them to a different restraint, with no questions it had the same wonderful view.

Lyka was doing her best to keep from being overwhelmed, but Tamra insisted on stopping at a Night club, this was where Lyka had a bite of trouble getting used to floating with a glass in her hand!

Qwe really got into the whole idea!

Chapter Thirty-seven

The travelers were greeting the morning with a larger variety of breakfast items around the automatic request table. With small conversation here and there, everyone was kind of feeling an itch to get on their way.

Entering the crystal room Emily & Lisa were explaining that not many people use this room because they didn't like the uncomfortable places they end-up, and what is the point of going to the future any farther?

For our group, it turned out to be about 200 years in the past of another world, but they didn't know that yet.

With everybody ready to go, Emily showed them the console and what to do,

"All of the modern traveling rooms are somewhat the same, so are you ready?"

She pushed a button on the console,
"See you in a few weeks!"

Phase out. … phase-in… same sort of room lots of crystals the four slowly moved through a small hall out into what looked like a marina, with a 200-degree view of an ocean - almost everywhere!

On this small island with a few buildings, there were lots of different sized boats in slips. As they walked out along a wooden boardwalk, there were few men behind a counter, and they took note of the four. Qwe walking up to inquire,

"Hello, we are sightseeing for a week, where is a good spot to start?"

"Kinda all the same, at least to us, that's why we rent old fashion fishing boats, but if you haven't been here before, go to the main square when you get down below. You will see a big kiosk that has all the information, and welcome."

With little interest,

Qwe, "Thanks, and the direction of the elevator?"

The man just pointed. Oz just nodded his thanks, and they found signs indicating the way underwater.

When the elevator door opened below, it was in the amazement of all; vast, huge clear domes let in quite a bit of sunlight at this 100 ft. level, without a doubt you knew you were underwater. — Flashes & flickers of sunlight all along the floor and walls, with a large variety of sea life swimming over head in the dome.

One of the things that struck them amusingly odd, there were palm trees underwater! Also, a public swimming pool with a sandy beach, tropical plants all over the place.

The pool had an infinite edge that made it appear as if you could swim right outside into the surrounding water!

Lyka had by that time just told herself

"I am just not going to be overwhelmed at anything anymore."

Tamra "Mom asked me to put my hands in some water when we got here, so give me a sec."

Sitting down on the raised edge of the pool, putting both hands in, first thinking "It's nice an' warm… hay 'lady…lake lady'...you around…? nope."

As she straightened up, she remembered the water must be fresh water, testing a finger, sure enough, it was saltwater. Back with the group and informed all,

"The 'lake lady' doesn't like saltwater."

Qwe then headed for the large kiosk wanting to find in what direction their hotel was. (Emily had made plans in advance) the kiosk attendant was accommodating and gave them electronic tags that would direct them,

"It takes about 10 mins. From here; your entrance to the tube that will take all of you down to that level is right over there, have a pleasant stay!"

Sliding into a clear cylinder car, they were taken on a very unusual ride through open Sea spaces between domes, through arches, down steep cliff faces. Lyka was trying to downplay the wonder, telling herself,

"No reason to get excited, there got to be something better than this, maybe...Wow!"

At the tube end, everybody enjoyed the ride so much they wanted to go again. Stepping out and into another large, manicured courtyard, following their locators, the hotel was found at the end of a short walk.

Everybody first wanted to freshen up and settle in their rooms. Looking at their options, and with little deliberation, they all took the hotel elevator up for dinner on the roof, without a roof. Each of the serving tables turned out to be a unique little floating island booth, step in to get situated, then the booth slowly floats randomly around the dome and randomly back down whenever your dinner is complete.

Tamra was wondering why Lyka was so quiet and asked if she could help,

Lyka "I will tell you when I get overwhelmed, trust me. Although, I'm almost there, Wow!"

Everybody laughs.

Tamra "Lyka ck. this out..."

She pushes a button on the menu, and a hologram of an attractive Italian waiter all of a sudden was standing right next to Lyka, "Vespere autem bonum fieri Voloservientes prymis ferculis Italicis."

Lyka now was staring with a frozen 'O' on her lips. Next, without missing a beat and a smile, she responded in 'Latin,' Flounder super lectum tuum a vapore aquae calidae Linguini cute quod gratias ago tibia."

With that, everybody broke out laughing again!

Qwe "Oh no, I was afraid this would happen, they look alike, and now Lyka is starting to take on Tamra's charm!"

Oz noticed the hologram menu, for ethnic waiter; you press a button as well for language.

[For the reader: She ordered "Fresh founder with a salad, and you are very handsome!]

It was decided they should seek out a public place tomorrow. Checking their jackets/coats holograms for any public gatherings or political events on the following day.

Qwe wanted to make sure everybody had a hotel locator along with the digital maps of where they were.
He asked them to split up once they got to wherever they were, stay out for an hours at a time then meet together at a common spot.

Their first stop was at the district union building, where a political speaker was holding an event regarding trading with other districts and the present overlords. This particular gathering wasn't huge, casually listening while each group wandered, looking at as many people without being rude.

After 4 hours, they all came to the same conclusion; this doesn't work. If Carisa had been taken twenty-two years ago for magic or just the fact of being a royal, she wouldn't be speaking for a crowd. Qwe had a thought, the lady at the large kiosk when they first arrived here was very nice, so they all took the tube back up to where they started.

The tube was just as amazing the second time on the up then down. Finding the kiosk and the same lady present, the question put to her was,

"Do you have a symphony or a ballet at present?"

"Why of course! We still enjoy the finer older things. Which would you prefer?"

Tamra didn't really like to go to either one, so she asked about plays "Is it possible that you have theatrical plays or some kind of acting for amusement?"

Kiosk Lady "Yes again! We all appreciate fine acting. Also, I will give your coats the directions with playbills that are current."

Qwe "Just for fun, what do the head's of government do for an outing?"

Kiosk Lady "Ha, good question, the heads of state change so often, it's difficult to keep abreast with it all, if you're looking to rub elbows with them now, try the racetrack. Horse racing is very popular here. I will give you directions; the best track is in D-8 leaving at the same station, there." Pointing.

Oz "Thank you very much, you will see us again!"

Tamra & Oz were very grateful they didn't have to hang out with the old "long hair's." Racing was something they all enjoyed, different and fun. Following the directions, they were given, found them in a lager tube which sat 15 in each car. This was the outer community transfer, the fluid motion was similar to a land train, each car moved a little different, which gave the ride a comfortable feeling.

Arriving about 15 minutes later they exited and followed signs to the race tube, they all happily jumped in. Ten minutes later, they were looking at what appeared to be a very familiar sight, and even the betting windows were similar.

Qwe looking at Tamra with a mischief's grin,

"Something wrong Tamra? Were you expecting 'Sea Horses?"

Tamra was deadpan,

"Hilarious dad, no, it just has so much the same, look, they even have racing forms that are printed. Hay! We don't have any money, how are we going to 'blend'?"

Qwe "Emily told me not to concern ourselves about that. It will be made up somehow. She gave me what looks like a credit card, here."

Tamra, "All right then! Let's get some racing forms and some seats!"

Qwe, "Let's try to get close to the private box seats if they have them and check the form for any kind of a schedule."

Oz found some close enough seats, they were taking in their surroundings, looking to see if they could buy a pair of binoculars. Oz noticed their table had a pop-up menu,

"It may be on here let's ck. yea, they have them, and all kinds of food & drinks, I'll go get everyone something if you want."

Qwe "Ok I would like a pair of looking glasses and a beer."

Tamra "You better hurry, says here the race schedule is 20 min between horses, I'll have the same, you need help? Oh boy! I haven't been racing in a year!"

Oz took orders and declined the help.

Qwe was looking at the well-dressed affluent people behind him hoping to see Carisa. His only guess was a possible look-a-like to Tamra or Lyka. Meanwhile, Tamra was explaining things to Lyka. She was getting an idea of the horse racing basics.

Post time was coming up, that got the two girls down to the betting Plaza windows. Tamra asked what an average bet was at the window, the man said 5 to 20 Supras, (equivalent to $25.0 to $100.0)

Tamra "All right then, ten on #6, and…"

…….Well, let me tell ya, it was a long afternoon…. Tamra was the only one betting after a while. It wasn't until the 8th race, she was standing at the betting window and decided to break up the monotony, thinking randomly "screw it, 1000 on #8" The man considered her,

"Are you sure, that's a real long shot, you are about the only one who put money on that sea anchor."

"Yep!"

And so, shaking his head, punching in her choice, then handing her the ticket.

Back at her seat, she told everybody else this was all she was going to bet, her last race, but didn't want to tell anyone how much she bet!

"It's ok, and I still had a nice time."

They scanned the crowd one more time…

"And away they go!"

Her attention back in the race halfway around, the crowd and the announcer were really getting into it, and it started to feel as if the stands were moving with all the people jumping up and down.

Tamra couldn't hear or see, the people in front were all standing yelling (they didn't seem happy) She listened to the announcer,

"Photo finish."

With that, the life of the crowd slowly began to quiet down for about 30 seconds,

" The winner is #8! …The amazing thing is folks; there are only four winners."

The whole crowd really didn't care and was sitting down. Tamra finally saw the #8 come up on the board, but that isn't what made her grab Qwe

"Dad! Look!"

It was pictures of all four winners, one of her, two of the other winners, the last was a picture of Anthony! The time hitchhiker.

Qwe stopped everybody,

"He's here! That means we are on the right track!"

Oz now had a gut feeling that he very much liked, now he had something to work with. Tamra told Oz she was determined to calm her prize so would he escort her?

Oz was looking very serious "You must be joking…"

Tamra "That was a line wasn't it, from one of his movies?"

"Ha ha yeah, give us two mins. Then go down to the betting Plaza, don't look for me, I gotcha"

With that, he and Art were gone, Qwe and Lyka looked worried.

Tamra "Don't give it a second thought, I am not worried, we have a set of snoops' on our side."

Lyka gave Qwe a strange look

Qwe just said with a smile,

"I'll explain later."

Down at the betting plaza, Tamra walked calmly, casually up to the same window, it was the same man,

"Hey lady, you need help spending that money?"

"Is it a lot?"

Man "You don't need to ever worry about anything anymore. You sure you don't want some help?"

"Thanks for the offer but can you just put all that in my act. And I need a receipt."

Man "Yes miss, it's already in your act, hay, the management wants to get pictures of you and the other winners."

Tamra "Nope… by"

Oz caught her eye and motioned her over around a corner. He asked her to go to the lounge with Qwe, Lyka, and Tayas. I am going to try and find the guy.

Making their way to the lounge and ordering some drinks, the group then waited. There was one more race, so people were heading out to trackside, leaving the room a little empty. While they were sipping their sodas, waiting for Oz, Tamra's coat started vibrating, touching her inside button and a hologram popped up, and it was Oz just speaking to her,

"You guys can hang-out for a while or go back to the hotel, I see him, and we are gonna follow him around."

Tamra told her group the guy was here, Oz and Art were following him, and we should head for the hotel. Lyka had a question for Tamra,

"You won money?"

"Yep, apparently I don't need to worry about working anymore."

Lyka, ''Wow!"

Tamra, "I know hu, Wow!"

Oz knew their surroundings were absolutely different, tracking like this without his own transport gave them some pause. Knowing that he would have to get very close to Anthony and somehow put a locator on him or one of his people. He had easily found him in what we would loosely call the "High rollers club."

Watching at a comfortable distance, he noticed Anthony very subtly sliding a small envelope into the hand of a fellow in his group.

Oz started followed that man for about five steps then that second man (b) tried to sneak it into another man, Oz and Art looking at each other almost started laughing out loud, these guys were so lame, this was to easy so far.

Oz again easily found Anthony sitting watching the last Race. He was surrounded with different people, thinking he might as well go for broke. Knowing the last time Anthony saw him was when Oz was covered with mud and dressed in rags, he got a drink and quickly moving in Anthony's direction, acting very drunk, muscled his way closer to the window, pushing and spilling vodka all over Anthony

"Ium suu scrrry "

Of course, Anthony tried to play it down,

"It's no bother"

Oz was trying to wipe the spill with a couple of torn napkins,

"suuurry I losoot moony."

Anthony "Fine, off with you!"

"okla, okl, Iana gooeen"

Staggering away, Oz & Art meet in a bathroom and straightened themselves up, then back to the Hotel. Tamra had a little surprise for Oz as he casually walked in,

"Hello how is everything?"

Tamra sauntered up to him

"Shaken not Stirred."

Handing them both a drink, gratefully excepting,

"I am starting to like the benefits."

As she sat down

"Did you guys shoot him, choke him, stab him look at him real mean, gerr!"

"That's funny ha-ha, well first, let's see who he is pretending to be today."

Taking a wallet out of his pocket and checking the interior,

"I see today he is going by the name of 'Alfred.'

Tamra "You stole his wallet!"

"Sure, it was easy."

Qwe, "I must say, maybe you are in the wrong line of work."

"Well let's see if this is going to help."

Opening all the interior sections and all it held was money from two other Worlds.

"Anybody have a clue? I have to get rid of this; anybody want to tag along?"

Tamra was taking Oz's arm,

"Dad, do you think it's safe to go outside with this guy?"

"Very funny, he'll do."

Oz "Thanks for the company, I want to take the tube up and dump it on top in case it has trackers on it, giving the idea that the thief left this Earth. Speaking of trackers, I put one on Anthony."

Tamra "Lead on Mr. Bond…"

On their little trip up and back, Oz was cautious of their surroundings, wandering slowly then dropped the wallet in the garden away from waste disposals spots. Tamra was going to ask but decided there must be a reason.

On the way back to the Hotel, Oz set his jacket to accept the signal from the device on Anthony. The hologram map popped up and,

"Apparently, he is still in District 8, doesn't look like a hotel, could be a private residence, I am not that familiar with the icons on this map."

Tamra "Why do you think that guy needed money, he can travel anywhere he wants, take anything he wants."

Oz "Remember when we were told about a crazy man who plays chess, real 3-D chess, I think that it was a strategic move to take the funds from someone else so that person couldn't use the money for whatever."

Tamra, "So, do you think I won that race because of magic?"

Oz "Kinda seems like it, I wonder if there is a way to block or check for magic."

Tamra "Sounds like a question for Merlin, and where is this Mr. Big madman anyway?"

"Well, maybe we can find him with the tracker on Anthony, the problem with this world is the lack of shadows for fading into and the physical access to places."

Tamra "Well I'm sure a famous someone would find a way, why can't you."

Oz "It'll happen, I hope."

The ride back down was still visually grabbing and had the two of them thinking about living here, nice and all, but they both decided they missed the beach and a good sunset.

Qwe and Lyka were talking about the floating restraint, Lyka was giving her coat a try at messaging and asked Tamra and Oz to meet them there.

Art and Oz were discussing Anthony and his location and what would be the location of the chess dude?

Tamra was steeping on to floating Island table, agreeing with Lyka that she could get very comfortable with having the evening repast while floating.

Upon the finish of their dinner and return of the table, a person was waiting for them. He introduced himself as a 'Runner' sent from the 'Paul' and asked them to step into a private room.

"Welcome, I was sent to inform you that what you have come to find is not on this planet. You may want to return to the world you entered from, or you may depart from this planet. The crystal that I have given Qwe will take you to the next water planet from this location.

There would be other 'Runners' looking for Carisa on that world and would get in touch with your group when you arrive."

Qwe and the others had decided to move on to the next world the following day, again, still not having an idea of how they were going to find Carisa.

Qwe, along the transfer process had a thought that they should hopefully try to see if the Symphony or some sort of entertainment was available when they arrive. Tamra chimed in and wanted to go to a high brow 'Broadway Play' if they offered them, then starting to wonder if there were such things here. Tamra had an idea that Qwe

& Lyka should go to the Symphony, and Oz and herself would see a play.

After getting settled back in their rooms, finding that there was in fact, nicer evening clothes, they all changed. And yes, they did find high-end amusement, so it was decided to have dinner after the entertainment.

Lyka asked what the' Symphony was and why Tamra so quickly volunteered for the 'Play.'

Tamra "Tell you the truth, I don't like the Symphony much, some people love it, and you being so old I thought…"

"What do you mean old!"

Lyka was standing her ground with her sister for the first time. Tamra, kind of surprised, not used to being questioned,

"You know, from an older time, you comedian you. I know you aren't 'old' we are twins."

Lyka "What is a comedian?"

"You know like a 'court jester' kinda thing."

"What's a Court Jester?"

Qwe, coming to the rescue of his two daughters

"Tamra, Lyka doesn't know what you are talking about because those two categories of people were before and after Lyka's historical timeline."

Tamra, "Ok, ok Lyka… which event would you like to go to?"

Admiring her fingernails, then casually looking at Tamra,

"The Play."

Tamra, with a determined scowl,

"If there were grass on the ground outside, I'd kick your butt!"

Lyka calmly looked at Qwe,

"Dad, is that like an invitation to the Colosseum"

"Yes, but not quite as serious."

Looking with a long even glair at Tamra,

"Your challenge is excepted."

Oz, "I 'll be sure to have the movie camera ready."

Small laughs all around.

That evening, Oz was happily amused at Tamra, she was mumbling under her breath while "enjoying" the performance, both looking through their opera glasses at the individual elevated seat placements.

Tamra whispered in Oz's ear, "let's split. It's half over I think…. Go"

She was relived just getting outside, heading for the floating table restraint. She wanted to leave a message with Lyka, for practice, talking out loud,

"This is your Loving sister; we got skunked!"

When she looked at her display hologram, it was Lyka,

"Tamra! SHE IS HERE! Fast as you can!"

Chapter Thirty-eight

Meanwhile, …let me bring you up to speed on things over at the Play,

'The Pleiades' (about a close-knit family of seven sisters with no neighbors that are close by) The production and the acting was fantastic! Qwe and Lyka were really enjoying themselves until Lyka noticed Carisa! She grabbed Qwe's arm and squeezed! She started to point up, but Qwe subtly eased her hand so as not to draw attention.

The production, being half over with, and their decision to leave wasn't favored by the audience as they excuse themselves from the 8th Row. Getting past all the sour looks and up to the mezzanine, while Qwe was trying to form a plan.

Qwe "It would be nice if Oz were here, the only thing I can think of is, let's wait on the mezzanine. Let's both send messages to them, maybe they will somehow answer."

While they were heading up the stairs, each was trying to send a message. Oz and Tamra were just entering the theater and noticed them on the stairs quickly as she could up behind and grabbed Lyka

"You saw her!"

"Yes, yeah! I can't believe it!"

Qwe was already on to explaining it,

"She is on the Mezzanine, stage Left, looked like there were four men and one woman in their group."

Oz "Thanks, oh, what does she look like?"

Qwe started to answer but Lyka stomped on his foot!

"Awwow!"

"Sorry dad!"

Lyka "Say you are sorry Tamra and I'll tell you."

"Now, for what!"

"Yes, say you're sorry…"

Tamra "FINE! I am sorry."

Lyka clapping and jumping up and down, grabbed Tamra and yelled,

"WE are Triplets!"

Art, Qwe & Oz were shaking their heads and looking at each other. Oz was developing more of a fast plan to get everybody out; he wanted Art and Qwe to watch the stairs on the other side,

"The girls are on their own kinda; you two need to keep an eye on all the stairs."

Oz eased over to the opposite side of the theater from where she was for an overview of everything, noticing there were two balcony exits. He moved around to her side, scanning for any other doors along the way, trying to consider the best approach. Should he move outside?

No, get behind the group, stay tight and watch for the right moment to move. He was hoping to get close enough to plant a locator, more natural with one of the men; he couldn't tell if Carisa had anywhere that would catch it on her dress. For now, just think and wait.

After the ovation, patrons were moving slowly towards the exits, Oz thought about somewhere on the stairs, so pausing halfway down, waiting along the side.

Descending the curved stairs with an elegant flair, his first thought when he saw her was, that's just like Tamra!

Noticing they did all three look very much the same. As she eased by him, she was looking down at the crowd, seeing something that made her stop mid-step as if she had seen a phantom, she froze.

Staring at two girls that looked just like her at the foot of the stairway, her company all pausing, the man next to Carisa noticed what she was looking at, and spoke to the three men quickly,

"Get those two" pointing at Tamra and Lyka.

It was then that everything started moving; the four men moved down and away from Carisa.

Oz knew his move was now, easily steeped in and taking Carisa by her arm, turning her, started back up the stairs. She began to resist. Oz noticed her still looking at the girls, talking at her ear in a quiet firm voice,

"They are your sisters; you are safe, come with me!"

She was in a little quandary; she did really want to be elsewhere from these people that had her captive now.

Deciding quickly to go with her new situation, stepped hastily up the stairs with Oz.

As all that was going on, Qwe and Art were on the far side of the Lobby, slowly making their way in and around the crowd towards the girls.

A large group of theater patrons started to move towards the exits. Part of Fidalac 's security team from the stairs had made it to Tamra & Lyka first. One man on each of the girls had them by their waist and forcing them towards a different exit.

Tamra had her hands free and decided to lift the man that had Lyka just enough, so he had no contact with the ground.

Lyka elbowed him on the jaw, pushing him away, that was sufficient for Tamra to throw the man down, then shove him into the crowd with natural hand movements.

She was really pissed off, with her arms free she was able to do the same with the man that was giving orders.

For fun she made him spin into the crowd, causing a large number of theatergoers to be quickly introduced to the ground.

As things moved on, another one of the men had grabbed Lyka and was being herded into the tube station. Oz was hanging on to Carisa so tight. She started hitting his hands

"Lay off! I am going with you!"

"Sorry, we gotta move fast, take you heals off!"

As they were trying to find another exit, she slipped them off and carried them.

Oz "Throw those away!"

Carisa "No you shit head, these come from another world!"

Oz, as they were dogging people,

"Just like my dear girl, to the point."

Carisa "We need to get out of here, where are you going."

Oz "Not now…. I need your sisters first. Stay with me close."

All this happened as they were heading down the opposite stairs, Oz was talking over his shoulder

"When we get off the stars, stay behind me I will explain later."

Now on the Concourse level, they meet with lots of people that were trying to exit the building, along with security people directing foot traffic. Oz took in as much as he could, then noticed Tamra across the room with a smile on her face. Qwe was almost with her, Oz not seeing Lyka, pushed across the foyer to meet Qwe and Tamra.

Oz "You hang on to Carisa and…."

"How did you know my name?"

Tamra, "I am a big hugging person, but later, I am Tamra your sister, you are going to love your story!"

Things on the Concourse were getting quite hectic,

Oz, "Not now, I need you."

"Au, he needs me."

Tamra said as he took hold of her hand and ran out of the building.

"This looks like your finger work, and we need it again"

Outside now they hurried to the tube looking for Lyka. What they found was another crowd standing back from the doors of the tube because they were on fire! Tamra kind of smiled,

"That's my sisters work!"

Oz "She does make it easy to find her, there, over by the kiosk."

Working through the crowd,

Tamra, "Very nice, good work! How did you dump the other two guys?"

"Those ugly dudes forced me in the Tube car, as they got in and were sitting down, I decided to set their paints on fire, and I think they are in the public pool over there! Thought I should cover that with a small fire around the tube!"

Oz "Tamra, even the 12 Th. century you is full of your mischief! Let's find the others and a different tube station, we need to head for the Hotel."

Turning away, they found two others that were roughly escorting Carisa heading straight for them and were definitely not happy; obviously, Qwe had been overcome and Oz quickly asked Tamra,

"Can you just shake the whole group?"

"I don't know, let me see…"

What she had on her mind was 'go away' so pointing three index fingers in a small spray, found the men and part of the crowd just slid backward, falling hard as if hit by high winds, Tamra picked Carisa up and got her on the move,

"That will do for a while, let's go."

Oz started to cut across a small park by the tube entrance by the public pool, and found the two sitting on the edge licking their wounds, noticing the girls they moved up to intercept, Tamra with a little smile,

"You two need to clean up more."

She picked them up and levitated them over the pool them dropped then in and out a few times then left them in the pool.

Tamra "Do you see dad anywhere?"

Oz "I hope he's headed back to the Hotel, let's fly that way ourselves."

Not actually flying but did get back quickly and were upstairs hoping the others had already arrived. When the door slid open, it was pandemonium! With everyone present, Art, Qwe & Oz decided to stand back and watch the sisters reunion. A smile was on every face, with of course plenty of tears.

Oz, after a short time was insisting on leaving as soon as possible, Qwe understood, so he had to step into his character as Dad.

"Girls, pack as soon as you can we have to hit the road! Oh Carisa, please leave all of your clothes here,

I'm sure one of your sisters has something your size, Oz is worried about being alive with bugs. "

Everybody decided to change, Lyka had a question,

"What does hit the road mean?"

All laugh, Tamra,

"We haft-a remember she is from 12 th century Rome,

Ha-ha, we gotta go!"

Chapter Thirty-nine

Fidalac was turning red, and violently uncontrollable. He couldn't form words, throwing things at his men. He wanted to know what seemed to make it so tricky for five men to hang on to one girl!

"One of the others used magic! We couldn't stand up, and one of them set us on fire!"

"All right! We know that! Does Carisa have her device on her?"

"Yes sir."

"Get everybody organized; I want all three of them! Come back here before you leave!"

Walking back and forth, throwing things, beating on furniture, threatening individuals in the group.

He was yelling at the top of his lungs for almost half an hour, lecturing anybody that happened to be within earshot. Finally, he told everybody to get out and get them!

Fidalac had talked too much, too long, and his men missed their chance of finding them.

Chapter Forty

Lyka "So what's it like living under water?"

She wanted to know about a lot of things about her new-found sister. The group had made it to the tube heading to the surface.

Carisa "Well, I am sure I love the water, but I really miss the beach, waves, and sunsets."

Lyka, "Oh, by the way, this is your father."

Tamra, "My turn, my turn and you are a Princess for real!"

As the Tube came to a stop, everyone out, Carisa was crying happy tears turned and gave Qwe a hug,

"Hi dad? we have some catching up to do!"

"Yes, dear girl, I can't wait for your mother to see you!" Heading straight to the crystal room, Qwe holding the crystal for Meyrim; Oz pushed the button, the musical hum started, and the travelers disappeared.

Phase in slowly it was dark in the Lab, Dr. J had no way of knowing when they were getting back. Qwe called Tayas, and what a surprise, she would be there in 10 mins, next calling Rym and Mera.

Tamra happily showing her sisters to the showers, putting some street clothes out for them, then joined them.

Oz & Qwe did the same thing, always nice to get the trip cleaned off.

Tayas ran into the lab not seeing anybody, so she went right for the shower, all three weren't even dressed yet, but Tayas walked up to Carisa and abruptly said

"Where have you been young lady!"

Hold it! (You say) Why did Carisa go with Oz in the first place? Sit back and let me fill you in.

She had been raised by a rich man and lots of servants she wasn't allowed out anywhere, with or without chaperones.

The servants were her only real friends, as she matured the Man only included her with him at political gatherings or banquets. Now, would you have stood in the middle of the stairs waiting for the three men to come back up or split with Oz? That's what I thought, split.

Carisa was naturally shy, not use to being found over lovingly. She embraced her mother for long moments, trying to recapture an entire childhood of hugs, with one good one. Then stepping back, she looked at Tayas closely

"Wait a while..., what's going on, you look the same age as I do?"

The other two sisters grabbed her hands,

Lyka "You won't believe it at first, then it gets terrific!"
Tayas took half-a step back with her arms folded,

"Who's doing the talking, you or me!"
Tamra "Sure bet mom, the floor is yours!"

By the time the Ladies emerged Rym & Mera were there, and Grand pop had his camera all ready.

Dr. J suddenly appeared, he said the silent alarm was going off in his apartment and was very happy to find the company safe and well with another addition!

It was a straightforward decision to place everybody together for the night and Tayas and Qwe had plenty of space.

Rym brought home Italian, and they were able to sit down for dinner as a family for the first time.
Carisa was having a troubling time looking for buttons or talking to nothing and expecting something to happen. Never having traveled very far, she found all that was surrounding her new and quite an adventure in a unique sort of way.

The girls from three different ages were attempting to share their inner young adult feelings with an actual family, for Lyka and Carisa for the first time.
Some small differences here and there, but the biggest wish for them all, was having their family all together.

To be loved as individuals in a family group was going to be so pleasantly new to them all.

Now, let's throw magic into the rendering.

Tamra wanted to get her sisters caught up on the not-too-distant past, and mentioning the 'Blue Lake' and the 'Lake Lady' (as she puts it) That brought up an instant reaction from Carisa,

"Can we go tomorrow? I love to swim! Let's go now … I know, I'll ask Tayas, or 'mom'"

Running into the kitchen and presenting herself a little out of breath,

"I'd like to go swimming…"

Tayas busy with letters and bills, "Sure, there is a pool over at the gym."

"Not that one, the Blue one!"

"Ha! Well, that's another 'trip to Europe.' Soon is our answer."

Carisa was a little unsure of the answer. She wasn't used to being turned down. But politely returning, and told her sisters,

"Mom said something like 'another trip to Europe' I'm not sure what that means."

Tamra "That means it's a long explanation and a lot of arrangements to be made. Don't worry, we get that all the time."

Chapter Forty-one

"This new twist has taken on a course of many different possible directions, and the next maneuver must be executed perfectly!"

Fidalac was pounding on anything he could reach again and yelling at the consortium that surrounded him.

"Let's review! There will be 25 armed men with Tasers close to the cave entrance HIDDEN! As soon as they materialize, handcuff everybody! Any of you dumb stupid shits don't get this simple set of directions!"

Anthony, "We all will follow through on those orders. Then we will split the three up again taking them to different worlds again you have specified."

"Stretch out the time difference on all of them. I am figuratively exposing my King and Queen on this game far too much. I want to be ready and be there two days before they leave that World they're on.

Are you receiving information on the bugs you planted when you were there in their laboratory?"

"Very clearly, just as you planned, we can hear the conference room and the lab."

"Tell me as soon as you hear anything more about it!

Chapter Forty-two

Dr. J, Dr. Rym, Dr. Qwe, and Oz started amassing a game plan, kind of upset with themselves for not making any formal big party plans for the return of the three girls. Another question was, who should stay here, who should go on the next trip. They could all go but how would they know if Merlin would even be anywhere close?

Qwe, at home that night discussing the problem with Tayas, as they were finishing the dishes,

"You know… I have your answer…Just take me over to Lake Geneva tomorrow, and I'll have a little chat with the Lady of the Lake."

Qwe "You are the clever girl! I didn't even consider that at all…again! Let me call Dr. J and agree on what is to be asked."

Tayas hadn't tried to find the 'Lady' yet here after her many trips, so she wasn't sure really if she could locate her.

Next morning, the Swiss weather was wildly rainy, large drops that completely saturated everything they came in contact with. Tayas & Qwe waited till noon to head over to Lake Geneva.

Finding a park with a small beach and a lot of tourists, she waded in a little then put both hands in the water.

The first few seconds she didn't hear anything, then weekly, slowly she felt her presence,

"Are you all here? Ma 'Lady we are in need to tell Merlin about our return trip and find out about a time to phase."

"Welcome your Highness; you have found your three daughters! And they are well?"

"Yes, it is wonderful! You will meet Carisa soon back in Alva glen, but for now, should we send Rym or Qwe alone?"

"I will convey your request to Merlin, arrive here tomorrow and I will have an answer."

Oz and Artemis having an interest in the welfare of the company, were at the Lab in a conference with Rym, as Tayas & Qwe came into the Lab, Tayas began telling everybody that the,

'Lady…" Oz started to talk over her and moving his index finger at a right angle across his throat,

"Huss" in a soft voice. Tayas was kind of looking between Dr.'s and shrugging her shoulders? Oz came over and whispered in her ear,

"Anthony left some bugs here, and the conference room, Artemus found them, let's move on to the hall."

All were stepping out and making sure the door was closed. Artemus explained that he had an electronic sweeping device and found two bugs, and they will have to move to another company meeting room. Keeping up a ruse that they need to act normal so as not to let the listeners think anything was amiss.

Tayas let them all know about the Lady and would know more tomorrow.

Merlin did, in fact, have much to say,

"Rym must see me before the whole company travels!"
He told Nyneve he would be at the castle for the next two days, then at Alva glen for a time.

Rym & Dr. J were going over the Hadron Collider test line-up schedule and had concluded that Rym could travel in four days.

In the meantime, Carisa, Lyka were attempting to learn English, Tamra was doing her best at writing things on a whiteboard.

"Do we have to learn English, why can't we just speak French?"

Tamra, "Well if you want to get a job across the street, you must speak French and English, that's it!"

Lyka "Speaking of that, what are we going to do about everything, School and where are we going to live?"

Lyka "Carisa, would you go back to living under water?"

"No, as I said, I miss the beach and sunsets way too much, I also like the mountains here, they are spectacular! I don't think I will go back underwater to live."

Tamra, "Lyka, you are from the 12 th century, no hologram handsome waiters, or buttons to push there, any ideas?"

Lyka, "I'm now very spoiled and won't be going back to Rome! Here, it is perfectly nice, all I need to do is learn English."

It was time for Rym to get on the phasing marks, Dr. J & Dr. Rym were planning on just two days with Merlin which should be enough. With the pleasant humming in semi-silence, the departure moved through smoothly.

Appearing back at Alva glen, Rym was happily meet by the very famous wizard with copious amounts of information.

"We must protect the girls, and my thinking is; the off-worlders could stage a surprise encounter here at the cave and capture you all.

I possess another crystal that comes from another small cave on the bank of the River Forth. That will make it quite a bit closer to Sterling castle and ultimately, Throne room."

"You, Qwe and Tayas by the way, will be crowned again along with your granddaughters. But first, we have to figure how to get them there."

Rym "Do the off-worlders have access to that many troops to engage in a larger war?"

Merlyn "They will bring what they need, there will be a limit to what they can do; still, it will include many. That is why we need to find all our people that are gifted.

We need to hold our ground until your Family coronation is done. Then all magic will be confined to this world, the Source world."

Rym, "Will, the girls be able to hold on to any gifts?"
"Possibly, for the three, but only in small amounts."

Rym "Should we stager the arrival?"

"No, we will have Alba, Rune and a lot of his fellows to meet you, then we must go as a group to the Castle.

Our Archbishop and Priests will already be in attendance, and it must be quick!

I have something special for Lyka, and Carisa, and should be in place before they arrive. "

He handed Rym two walnut boxes with three gold bands around the top of each one, like the one he gave to Tamra. So it went, all through the night they would toss ideas back and forth, the next day they felt their plan was something they could work with.

Chapter Forty-three

The next afternoon after Rym arrived back in Meyrin, Switzerland everybody started talking with their hands in the lab due to the bug. That was getting old, so it was decided a neutral location for everyone over at Qwe & Tayas's that night for more fine tuning of the whole idea, and again R-4 Italian for all.

The company would travel in two days. Rym was giving them all and any information that he could think of regarding the instructions of Merlin.

Oz was really having a dilemma with how much tech to bring along, and with all the ammunition it was getting somewhat heavy. Qwe was polishing his Saber and was getting a feeling of pre-fight energy.

Tamra was putting on fingernail polish, Lyka and Carisa were wearing their crowns (Qwe had officially crowned each one already.)

Rym told them there would be no time to change when they arrived so we all will look the best we can when we all leave.

Chapter Forty-four

The company had a cast of nine, Mera had informed Dr. J that she had phased with groups about that size, so as no concern. Tayas asked Dr. J, if he would take a picture for the history books, yes, of course, was his answer.

Qwe, "Only problem being, whose history books are we going into!"

Rym, "We have one minute …"

The Machine started it's very pleasant humming, soft vibrating then the start of the out of focus phasing …out…

The banks of the River Forth on a cold, drizzly morning came into focus with Merlyn and his company close by.

Merlin "No time to talk now (in a quiet voice) come along with me. "

Everybody quickly fell into line and followed him into a small glen with maple trees and hawthorn bushes all about. The walls of the little glen were slowly rising.

After a time, they came upon a pile of medium size rocks at the foot of a significant cliff. Merlin held out his Staff and uttering a spell; the rocks moved willingly aside. Ushering all inside he again closed the rock group, erasing traces of footprints in the sand and rock with small hand movements.

Gathering everybody around, he lit a torch then asked Tayas to lite some more. Tamra started to help but…

Merlin, "Not just yet Tamra, soon dear girl, I've seen your work…"

"We will move along this tunnel for a time when we come to stairs that lead into an anti-chamber off the Throne room."

Spacing themselves out to easily see the dirt footpath with their torchlight, Tamra grabbed an unlit torch and lit it herself just because of his remark. Tayas just passed her by laughing and smiling, shaking her head.

Almost at the Throne room, they started to hear lots of commotion,

Merlin "Listen: <u>You must think like a Rock</u>! Do not in any way let any of the noise or flying objects distract you. I have a protective spell that surrounds all of you. The bishop and lesser Royal families are in place now. I will let them know we are all here."

All three Princesses gave him the strangest look,

Lyka "I'm going to have too ask you about that later…"
Merlin "Yes later! Do It!!!"

When he opened the chamber door, truly the noise was almost overwhelming! The bishop motioned them all forward; Merlin was placing everybody, then quickly asked Oz & Art to move off to the other side of the room. The bad guys were easy to spot, pointing verbalizing some kind of lousy oath. The two needed no coaching, both eagerly drew their 9 mm, screwing the silencers on and started their defense. A quick "Proof, Proof."

Bad people with swords and spears were always falling down with confused looks on their faces, "Proof" another one, here comes one "Proof" that one fell down also, this was getting like the moving target range back home! At times they felt the gun being pulled from their hands, he & Art had practiced that very thing. Tamra could almost remove the gun with her new gifts, but with Tayas trying, they only felt a noticeable tug.

Merlin was standing on the left of the group, extended his arms outstretched with his staff in one hand then everything stopped!

The sound was no more except that of the bishop. People tried to cast spells, but nothing happened. When they did there was a funny sound "proof," and then somebody else would fall over, they couldn't figure that out.

The coronation was less than 5 mins. Oz noticed Merlin's arms starting to shake under some kind of strain. He moved to the other side of the room, two guys on the way towards him 'Poof poof' just fell over. Reaching Merlin and lifting his shoulders from behind seemed to help.

Merlin, "Thank you ma boy the spells of many are heavy, get the company and move them back to the anti-chamber!"

Moving quickly up to the Dais, gathering the three look a likes, hastily getting everybody back in the room.

People kept falling over in Oz and Art's wake, with that same look of confusion.

The noise again was elevated again as they passed Merlin, he shut the door and order were restored in the anti-chamber.

Rym, "It was my impression that when we were crowned, the wrong would be righted!"

Merlin, "No, the battle rages all along the outer wall, along with A good a number here on the inside. Our coronation is not complete; we must pass through the Throne room to the Royal receiving balcony for the review of the crowd."

Qwe, "That seems out of the question at the moment, even with Oz and Art pressing the lead!"

Merlin, "Quite … I have a thought; We must talk to the 'Lady of the Lake!' Come along now."

The Company was quickly ushered along halls and rooms, then to their surprise, out into a medium-sized courtyard with a fountain and a sizeable pool around it. Merlin, kneeling at the pool put his two hands in and,

"My dear Lady are you present? (Small pause)
Nyneve, "Yes my Merlin, I'm always with you."

Merlin, "MA' lady we are in a pressing need, I plan to take the company down to the Kings Knott to draw the fight in that direction!"

(For the reader, The Kings Knott and Jousting field are just below to the West Southwest of the Castle and are there to this day.)

Nyneve, "I will help, but two of your group do not have that gift."

Merlin, "Yes I am aware, and will inform them. Thank you."

Addressing the group, he gave them all of his plans and informed Oz & Art that they could not follow, but to stay here. They would return the same way after a time. Some of the others objected but, Tamra,

"Are you kidding, worried about J. B. and his buddy! The only thing you have 'a worry about is running out of bullets! And even then, I am not worried."

Oz, "Thank you for your confidence, Tamra."

Tayas, "Carisa, I need to tell you about Nyneve."

Carisa, "Lyka told me all about her! I have been waiting!"

Merlin, "Everybody let's get in…"

Each member waded in turn, Tayas went before Carisa to Introduced her to' Nyneve.'

Tayas, "MA' lady, my daughter Carisa."

Nyneve, "Welcome, not a time to talk now we must leave, would you like another breath?"

Carisa, "No thank you! I am very much at home here."

Nyneve, "A girl after my own heart!"

The sight must have been very odd to fish and frogs seeing a string of humans disappear into the water source on the bottom of the pond. And it was extraordinary for the humans to be passing down through fishers of spring water to find themselves an arriving in a sizable, elongated pond. And as quickly as they entered, they exited.

Merlin, with a chant and a wave of his staff and a small wind, all things were dry!

Merlin "Tamra it's your turn, would you be so kind as to lite a fire off there in the field."

Tamra, "Cool, anywhere?" [Yes!]

Rubbing her hands together, pointing with two fingers of each hand, concentrated then spread her fingers and "vwwwwoooofff"

A giant vacuum of air about them suddenly rushed past the group then the field was filled with flame!

She was still pointing at the sizable field which completely lit-up!

Tamra, "Now that's a WOW!"

Merlin, "I mentioned it would be your turn soon, not to bad!"

Carisa gave Tamra hi-five!

Lyka stopped, with a scrunched-up nose looking the two girls like, what the hell was that about?

Here they were, standing on a raised circle of green earth with a vast field surrounding them and a giant fire in one of the tracks behind them.

Merlin's thought was to hopefully draw the main body of the enemy down to this location with the intended smoke; it's about 600' up to the Castle from here so it would take the opposing side a little time to regroup. He was also hoping that people from the Village of Sterling, which is very close by would come out to investigate the fire and be ready to fight!

Qwe "This looks so different now, being here at the time they actually, use this field for jousting."

Tayas "You like this kind of stuff; would you really get on a horse with a stick and ride down some other guy right here?"

Qwe, "Now that I am here, I'm not too sure."
To the delight of Merlin, men were starting to come around from town. Merlin was again hoping that whoever was leading the attack, would see the townspeople and think that we are trying to make our public appearance down here to consummate the coronation.

Merlin called some of the village people over to warn them they would be leaving soon, be on your guard for the enemy! Things took about an hour to redirect at the Castle. Now spells of noise and anything not nailed down came their way. Anybody in the company that could repel things with their finger spells did!

Chapter Forty-Five

Now with Oz and Artemus up in the castle not used to watching events go bye, feeling they had to do something for the good of the cause. So, the two came up with a plan that they were pleased with. Athena, Oz sister, had shown the boys a lot of tunnels and back hallways.

First off, they found their way to one of the turrets of the castle for an overview; they needed to locate the base of operation for the enemy. In the tower, they discovered a significant concentration along the South, which really is the only way to approach the castle in force. Noticing at the rear some standards which gave both a perfect idea.

Running back into the heart of the castle, they knew of another way in and out on the West slope, very steep more accustomed to rock climbing. It was used in time of siege to get messages to other forces for assistance. Art was thinking; they would traverse around to the South, skirting the main troops, moving to the rear, then get within pistol range of the command post if possible.

Already having been in that part of the woods this morning with the company at Merlin's tunnel, that gave them both a better working knowledge of the surrounding woodlands.

The afternoon had brought a lite rain and a strange fog that lingered long in strange thick fingers.

That helped, but the rain didn't. Moving out of a tiny window and on to the rock face, with rain falling lightly is no fun with hundreds of feet to the ground below.

The two boys were reminded of what they used to do, keeping three points of contact on the wall, it wasn't vertical but close enough.

That made it a little harder because you must drag your bodies weight along the rock. It was a long wet 100' + - climb/traverse. Concentration is critical, and it served them well as they stepped off into the forest edging low, fading Into the back drop of maple trees, oak and birch.

Working their way to the South, along Into the glen, finding the object of their interest. Art had a single lens sight glass with him, and glad he did. His focus landed on the profile of Anthony, now acting General for Fidalac . Oz quickly searched for a closer position, noticing that Anthony's offense was mostly forward and right of the center, possibly to deflect magic from the direction of the castle.

Slipping through the hawthorn bushes which thankfully added to cover, they could almost hear Anthony's panicked voice he was yelling so loud. He was getting the news that Merlin had changed the rules of engagement.

Slowly moving with the cover of large rocks carefully closer. For about five minutes they listened to him tell everybody around him that he was going to kill them if they didn't do what he ordered now! Oz, Art listened carefully, another minute… Anthony observably hyper, took out a knife and stabbed somebody close to him! Then, launching into another verbal tirade with more threats of violence and death.

Oz, whispering to Art, both guys with guns out and getting in a better position,

"Art, I'm gonna help these guys out…Puuouf, Puuouf, Puuouf!

That last shot was just to make sure!"

Art "I'll do em another favor."

His aim was lower and closer to guards that may become a problem following them.

As quickly as they could, quietly moving off to a different location, stopped and listened to the pandemonium. They both were satisfied with the monkey wrench they through Into the mix, and began retracing their steps back to the castle.

Two hours had passed, and Merlin had tired of keeping the protective bubble in place around the Company, Rym was getting tired of holding Merlin's arms up. Qwe finally was able to engage in some sword work, he made it look easy having studied the subtler points of fencing.

The momentum of the small battle started to move away from the water, they all needed to stay back close to the little Lake. Tamra began to throw two lines of fire in the direction of the lake to clear the way.

While the village men and women were fighting with their swords and rocks against the enemy, the company quickly and comfortably moved straight into the water one after the other as Merlin brought up the rear.

Turning to extinguish the flames in the field, then hurled some leftover burning ashes at a large group of the enemy trying to slow them down.

Arriving together with the Lady of the Lake up at Sterling castle, once out of the water Merlin dried everybody off once again and immediately led the company back through to the anti-chamber.

Where they found Oz and Artemus out in the Throne room, very casually sitting on the King and Queen's thrones, shooting anything that looked ugly. That made It really easy; most all these people were historically really ugly!

At the sight of Merlin and Rym, they both jumped respectfully up fast as they could, while still keeping an eye on the approaching bad guys,

Oz "Sorry ah, Sorry your Majesties."
Qwe, giving it his Kingly best trying to look concerned,

"That tizz a Nobel effort in the service of we Kings and Queens. I see no error done…continue on where you let them drop!"

With a profanatory wave towards those that wished them ill will, He motioned Oz and Art to continue on…. please.

Tamra could not contain herself; likewise, the whole company burst out laughing!

Merlin, "Not yet my Kings, Queen, and Princesses! Now is the time! Fast as possible!"

All running as fast as they could with Oz leading and Merlin and Artemus trailing. Art was backing up and shooting with his two pistols, then moved up with Oz to break out onto the balcony.

They meet five or six with swords, and with all their 9mm at a full run clearing the stairway. Changing clips and running head on to the balcony where they meet five men.

All with similar weapons, a small exchange of a few shots, then Tamra who was directly behind Oz.

Sidestepping and around the boys with both hands extended, she willed all five in a tight bunch and lifted them out over the receiving square, shaking vigorously they dropped what they had in their hands and were grabbing on to each other for dear life!

Merlin was first to approach with his staff, commanding them as they hung in space,

Merlin, "You have lost your purchase here on this Earth, you can no longer export magic of any kind."

Fidalac , in a very panicked voice,

"I think we need to be put down, and we can talk. My name is Fidalac …"

Merlin, slowly reciting and lifting his Staff, then silence again.

"You are no longer to ever be present in this world at any time in the past, present or future. We have followed ancient law, and by all the Royals standing here at this moment, and the fact of your silence indicates you and your people no longer have that power. You must be gone in seven hours from this moment!"

Tamra didn't want to be troubled with any of "Those shit heads"

With both hands for fun turned them upside-down! Then holding them thus, she moves them out over the drop off (1000') and kept them there.

Tamra "Hay Merlin Sir, I see the Forth River, is it too far away for me to give these assholes a bath?"

Merlin "Yes, it is, but if I may help, we together can accomplish your request!"

Tamra "Wow! Me and Merlin are doing magic, that's what I'm takin about, yes that would of great help, that mess is getting heavy."

Merlin "All right, away with them down to the river!" Yelling their heads off, slowly drifted down towards the river, and at a somewhat uncomfortable height above the water, Qwe, jokingly,

"Now princess, don't play too mean!"

Tamra, "Don't worry Dad, au, Your Majesty aa, Sir, I wonder if I can make them drop just a little... (At that, Merlin just gently pushed her arms down a little)

"Wow! Listen to that! They really know how to scream like little girls! Ok, ok I'll put them upside-down and in the middle of the river! I don't care if you fuck heads don't know how to swim!"

"That's getting off easy you assholes! You should be dead for tearing our Family apart!"

Merlin "Very nicely placed! Wow!"

Fin.

(Maybe)

EPILOGUE

A warm Swiss summer late afternoon lent itself willingly to a family barbecue in the backyard with grappa Rym & Mera and Dr. J; you would think it would be peaceful place... Nope,

Tamra "Look, you two, don't you get it! I am the Boss!"

Lyka "You are so far out of touch! You're not the boss of me!!"

Carisa "Yeah! Bark at the Moon!"

Lyka "Yah, don't forget to roll in the mud after you do that!"

Tamra "You two just called me a dog! I feel a colosseum event coming on!"

Tayas standing with an arm around Qwe at the B-B-Q

"Isn't it amazing that one of those girls has a PhD Mathematics, one is from the 12th century, and one from the future was raised mostly underwater. Yet they still fight like they have been here and together all their lives, I love it!"

Qwe "It oddly does feel like home, and I love it."

Dr. J "It does appear that they have taken nicely to each other, and I will have to chuckle a little on that far reaching thought according to some people that don't know them."

Taking a deep breath,

"I am wondering how I am going to put all this in an 'Anthology of Physics ' with some kind of added poetic explanation."

Tayas "We could just historically forget it ever happened..."

Qwe "Hum, I would think......."

Dr. J was interrupting "You truly cannot be serious, with all our background and our endeavors Dr. Tayas!"

Tayas "Maybe, I just wanting to avoid all the publicity."

Qwe thoughtfully considering,

"Talking about the publicity, I do wonder about going down that alley."

Dr. J "It would take all of you out there and come to think of this aspect of your situation, your whole family was born in the time of Merlin. That means all of your twin selves are here; there are many factors of course. If we do go public, there is a risk of meeting yourself and canceling yourself out!"

Qwe "You bring up a big problem, not only with our family but where was Fidalac from originally?"

Tayas smartly "I vote for no public!"

Qwe "I will happily change stances and agree, let us let sleeping dogs lie…"

Dr. J "This is only a distant possibility… but yes, let's let it rest. There is too much at stake, I'm enjoying watching the girls interact with each other and I wouldn't want to change that."

That put the three of them too laughing; It was even enough to sidetrack the girls bantering interchange amongst the three for a breath or two!

Fin

(For now)

ACKNOWLEDGMENTS

I have to Thank my brother Dave who introduced me to science fiction at an early age, also his encouragement on all of my efforts.

My amazing father & mother would have been 'thunderstruck' if they were able to see my name on a book I authored.

My father, who kept telling me…

"Never Limit God!"

Thanks to all of you who took the time to muddle through this.

Please let me know what you think!

Jon Shaw:

nextaddress100@gmail.com

ABOUT THE AUTHOR

Born and raised in San Diego, as the youngest member of a pastor's family, an older brother and my tireless mother.
As a family, we all were able to live in Coalsnaughton, a village in Clackmannanshire, Scotland north of Sterling for a long summer. I was at the age of twelve and fell in with the village boys/girls making mischief with all the beautiful countryside had to offer.

Subsequently, another extended European holiday visiting notable people, and interlacing places all across the content.

Not finishing college, the lure of tangible's took me into a G-construction license.

Married and was blessed with triplet girls, who now are about to finish what their father didn't.

My out of door actives took-in a wide spray of surfing, skiing, moto-cross, rock climbing, diving, trekking, and flying.

I can't go anywhere without mentioning my life long family of friends, they are responsible for helping me through all my years.

Presently single, happily retired and living in Hawaii.

ALSO, BY

JON W. SHAW

Annotated Notes in Time:

Book 1. **EARTHS** -
Invisible Presence

Book 2. **LINGERING EARTHS** -
A Precipitous Presence

Book 3. **ENDURING EARTHS** -
A Propitious Presence

And...

-STEMMING TROUBLE©
Science Adventure

-In A Blue Moon© Adventure

Due out in 2021

AFTER A BLUE MOON #2

Artificial Horizons #2

Referenced Papers or Publications :

JOURNAL ARTICLE
Merlin and the Ladies of the Lake

ANNE BERTHELOT
Arthuriana
Vol. 10, No. 1, ESSAYS ON MERLIN (SPRING 2000)

Mary Stewart: The Arthurian Saga

From Myrddin to Merlin and Back Again:
  Stephen Knight, MA, PhD

Made in the USA
Columbia, SC
28 January 2022

54882827R00140